PENGUIN BOOKS

VIRTUAL CENTRE AND OTHER SCIENCE FICTION STORIES

Raissa Falgui's fiction has been published in various anthologies: "The Sorceress Queen" in *Alternative Alamat*, "Dreaming of the Sea" in *Of Words and Water 2014*, and "Light in the Water" in *Likhaan 8*. Her stories have also appeared in *The Philippine Graphic*, including "In the Dark Zone" which was a third prize winner of their 1999 contest. She has also published a young adult historical novel, *Woman in a Frame*, which was a finalist for the 2015 Philippine National Book Awards and winner of the 2013 Filipino Readers' Choice Award for fiction. Her other published books are children's picture books: *Hating Kapatid*, *Bilangan sa Karagatan*, and *A Boy of Buhi*. She is a graduate of the University of the Philippines with a BA in Art Studies and an MA in Creative Writing.

Virtual Centre
And Other Science
Fiction Stories

RAISSA CLAIRE R. FALGUI

PENGUIN BOOKS
An imprint of Penguin Random House

PENGUIN BOOKS

USA | Canada | UK | Ireland | Australia
New Zealand | India | South Africa | China | Southeast Asia

Penguin Books is part of the Penguin Random House group of companies
whose addresses can be found at global.penguinrandomhouse.com

Published by Penguin Random House SEA Pte Ltd
9, Changi South Street 3, Level 08-01,
Singapore 486361

First published in Penguin Books by Penguin Random House SEA 2020

Copyright © Raissa Claire R. Falgui 2020

ISBN 9789814882972

Typeset in Adobe Garamond Pro by Manipal Technologies Limited, Manipal
Printed at Markono Print Media Pte Ltd, Singapore

www.penguin.sg

To those who gave me space and time (to write)—Joel, the Cat, the Cub, and the Sage.

Contents

1

Virtual Centre

Delia stepped onto the escalator leading to the MRT as she did every morning. Beside her, robots were making adjustments to the down escalator. As she ascended, she thought how lucky she was that robots could not do the work she was doing now, had been doing for the past twelve years, ever since she graduated from high school. She shoved her pass into the turnstile and pressed a button to indicate her destination. The Centre, of course, as it was for virtually everyone else. The turnstile beeped, flashed that her ticket was accepted and that the corresponding amount of money was deducted from her account. She was lucky to find a seat on the train.

She remembered her first trip on this train as a tiny child of three. Her mother had taken her, and they had gone to visit her grandmother in the hospital. There were just as many people then but maintenance robots were just starting to be used. And there were the same number of stops but more people got off at every stop. Now, everyone who got on was headed for the Centre for work. After work, a few went shopping. Delia went occasionally herself, but she avoided the malls when she was low on cash. That was the trouble with paying for everything with a debit card. You could use up your money quickly if you weren't careful. The debit card machines showed you exactly what your account balance was every time you paid, but some people, like her friend Mariel, never learned and sometimes had to go through the hassle of refunding an item or applying for credit. Interest rates were so high that credit wasn't worth it. If you tried to leave without paying, the security cameras would record your transgression and the authorities would shut off your access to your bank account until you returned to the store and paid. It was a foolproof system. Children who didn't have debit accounts would find their parents contacted by the authorities. Delia used to think, when they introduced the system in high school, that it would never work. A person could simply hide their identity by disguising themselves and never be caught, right? She found out otherwise when her brother Nick and a couple of his friends tried shoplifting wearing hooded sweatshirts and bandanas covering most of their faces. The exit beeped a warning and the glass doors slid shut, entrapping all the young miscreants, except her brother, who managed to dash through. Her father had received a letter and pictures that informed them that their son had shoplifted, and if he did not make restitution he would have a criminal record and his guardians would have restricted access to their bank accounts. Nick returned the silver bracelet to the store and never again tried to steal. He figured that the store cameras had X-ray vision. And the government's computers, their father told him, had records of every person in the country, which had to be updated every year if they wanted to have access to their money.

Money really talked nowadays, in a way it hadn't when they were young children. Life certainly was much better now than it had been in their parents' youth. Delia's heart ached for her mother, who had been the valedictorian of her high school class but got pregnant and couldn't go to college. Instead, she worked in the best job she could get without higher education. She took care of a rich family's children all her life and died miserable over not having been able to truly utilize her potential. Her husband worked as a delivery truck driver for very low pay. Of course, such jobs were obsolete now. Only the poor had children now, and computers had replaced human drivers just as they had replaced factory workers.

At the next stop, she saw Mariel through the window and waved at her. She wasn't sure Mariel had seen her, but it didn't matter as she knew where to look for Delia. Mariel squeezed into the seat Delia had saved for her. 'Where's your brother?' she asked Delia.

Delia threw up her hands. 'On strike. Rebelling as usual, even if nobody's following him anymore.'

'Why should anyone rebel?' Mariel said. 'So maybe our lives aren't as great as those of the people we take care of. But we certainly have things a lot better than our parents did. At least everybody has a job.'

'He sometimes tries to talk me into going off with him and living off the land on our own.'

'Crazy talk!'

Delia had to smile. Then she added pensively. 'If my father wasn't ill and in the hospital, maybe we could. He grew up on a farm so I suppose he knew something about growing food. Not that he would have wanted to go live in the wild.'

'Why would he? Our work may not be exciting but things are easier this way.'

It was true that everyone had work, despite the fact that everything else was automated—not only factories but just about everything else. Banking was now all done by machine, and vending machines and online stores had completely replaced actual shops. Even delivery vehicles roamed the streets with no drivers, once programmed by the few human staff members assigned to these tasks.

Since the government restricted access of all provisions and privileges to those who worked and those who had worked and retired at the appropriate time, the only way one could possibly avoid depending on the government for one's daily bread was to go to the few wild spots left and live off the land. But few people knew how to do traditional farming anymore. It was something you read about in history books. Computers and robots took care of cultivation and processing these days. Who would want to work that hard? If you weren't a government official or skilled programmer, it was better just to work in virtual care like they and most of the population did. Delia didn't mind but she couldn't soothe Nick's complaints.

'Nick complains it's just like in our grandparents' time. There's class division. And there's no way out of it unless you can afford to pay someone to take care of you for life. And that they pay us just enough to feed and clothe us and transport ourselves to the Centre, so we're never going to be able to break out of the cycle.'

'Well, that's just how things have been throughout history,' Mariel said. 'Don't tell me he's becoming a Marxist like those people back in the 1960s, or was it the '70s? My God, that was a hundred years ago! And they didn't accomplish anything, did they?'

Delia just nodded. She didn't let Mariel into her thoughts. She was remembering Reggie, her first and only love. He had big dreams. He wanted to start a new society, free from their government. He had tried to escape to the mountains. He had asked Delia to come with him, but she was frightened and refused. A few weeks later, his lifeless body was shown on the evening news, next to the makeshift vehicle he had created, which had somehow caught on fire. Nick hinted darkly that he was attacked by the robotic patrol helicopters but Delia was sure it was an accident. One man alone seeking freedom wasn't a threat to society, was he?

The train was growing increasingly more crowded and even though Delia hadn't been paying attention to the number of stops, she knew they were close to the Centre. She looked out the window and saw Manila Bay, greyish and murky beneath her. She saw the Centre, a massive dome of interwoven steel rods and glass, appropriately looking not unlike a greenhouse. And then the train slowed to a stop and the recorded voice announced: 'Virtual Centre Station.' Delia and Mariel got off the train, strode off with the tide of workers, put their cards through the turnstile and retrieved them, then stepped on to the moving walk that conveyed them to the Centre itself. They entered their identity cards through another turnstile. The steel door opened to the large ward. And they went to work in an enormous room with a domed ceiling. Its temperature was nearly freezing, despite the sunlight filtered through the mirror-tinted glass. It did not have the temperature of a greenhouse but it was like a greenhouse nevertheless, for it was here that bodies were cultivated.

The room was filled with people's bodies strapped on chairs that belonged in the dentists' offices of old. They were fitted with masks, wires, electrodes, IVs, and feeding tubes. They reminded Delia of her grandparents on life support machines in the hospital after they had strokes or heart attacks, of her mother in the last days before she succumbed to kidney disease. Except that these people were not ill. They were the very rich who had given up on ordinary living and were living a virtual life. The masks on their faces were supposed to project images they watched, images corresponding to the type of life they wanted to lead. Electronic impulses gave them the appropriate sensations. Even their tongues had electrodes on them to stimulate taste. Delia and Mariel's job was to check on their bodies during their waking hours. They were programmed to sleep at a certain time of the night, and to wake up and experience their virtual lives at 9.00 a.m. every day. The caretakers monitored the individual bodies, watched for signs of distress, listened to their requests (Delia's body often had a craving for pizza), and inputted these into the computers by the bedside. They also observed them for any symptoms of illness or deterioration though, in this capacity, they were really only a back-up to the more reliable electrodes and cameras. Bedsores were prevented by the special cushioning of the seats.

There was really not much work to do but no one shirked or moved from their place until the bell rang in the evening. They were paid to stay there all day, making sure their particular charges were happy and healthy. They could not die if they were cared for properly. If one happened to die, then the income of that body's caretaker would be terminated. Mariel called hers DOM (for Dirty Old Man), though his name, as indicated on the plate on the back of his seat, was Roberto Paez. She often blushed while at his side, watching and listening. 'Why couldn't I have gotten a woman?' she often asked Delia. The girl working on Mariel's other side had the luck of having a former movie star. They often laughed at her antics. She was always going to the beauty parlour and tossing her head and she would sometimes scream or cry alarmingly, but they soon realized that she was imagining herself acting in a film. Delia had one of the youngest, a man who had been a famous singer in his youth. She remembered watching him on TV when she was little. He looked about her age, even though she knew he was at least ten years older. In their refrigerated climate, protected from the stresses of daily living and pumped full of hormones, the bodies hardly seemed to age.

She smiled at her ward, even though she knew he couldn't see her. 'Hello Art,' she said. He was humming and moving his fingers as if playing a guitar. He did that a lot. The man beside her muttered, 'I don't see how he could have become rich as a singer. I'm glad I have a quiet religious woman to work on.' But Delia liked Art's voice. She remembered how, like most girls, she'd had a crush on him back in high school and was devastated when he chose to retire to the Centre. She couldn't believe her luck when she was assigned to him.

Behind her, her brother's friend Bert was instructing a substitute on caring for Nick's body, the body of an ex-politician who often startled them by uttering slogans in a loud voice. Nick often complained about his dull speeches riddled with clichés. The new apprentice jumped back in surprise as the politician suddenly stretched out his hand. 'You don't have to shake it,' Bert assured her. 'The electronic gloves take care of making him feel the pressure. The electrodes send the message to the glove that he imagines he's shaking someone's hand and that's when he feels it. Your job is to detect signs of complex emotions, mostly negative ones, and input them and your recommendations for relieving them. You have the emotions and symptoms charts?'

'Yes.' She held up a folder which showed different facial expressions and gestures and the corresponding emotions that they could be symptomatic of.

'We veterans don't bother with that anymore but you'd better refer to that now and then,' Bert advised. 'Any questions?'

'Yes,' said the girl. 'If the support system is programmed to make their lives go the way they want it, how come they still feel unhappy sometimes?' Bert whistled. 'That's a tough one. Well, I think it has to do with hormones, and that what they want changes, and sometimes it has to do with the fact that some people like to feel pain, like this old lady. She's always complaining that something hurts, and I input that into the computer, then she says, 'Thank you, hijo,' or 'That's my good girl,' or something like that. In the profile they gave me, there's this essay she wrote where she says she wants to be in a virtual world where her children won't leave her and will take care of her all her life.'

'Oh,' the girl said. 'What problems does this man have?'

'He gets into loud arguments once in a while and the computer sets it up so he wins.'

'Mine is pretty happy,' Mariel said, 'as long as he's having sex. Though he gets into arguments with his jealous girlfriends once in a while. He likes making them jealous! The computer sets it up so that they always forgive him and come back to him. Delia's seems happy all the time.'

'He gets frustrated sometimes, though, when a song he's practicing doesn't sound right to him,' Delia told them. 'The computer works it out so that he gets distracted from the song. There are some things the computer can't do, like make a song sound perfect. Not when Art himself doesn't know how he wants it to sound.'

Art was making slurping sounds as he had his breakfast. He reminded Delia of Nick when he was a baby.

Bert didn't seem surprised that Nick wasn't around. Maybe Nick had told him about his plan. But Delia didn't want to ask Bert about it in front of everyone. Someone might report him. Nick had already been in trouble for rebelling against the system, back when he was a senior in high school. Delia was already working at the Centre then. Nick questioned her constantly about her job. Then one day their dad had gotten a note from his social studies teacher complaining that the boy was always challenging the system. Their father had talked to him, and Nick had subsided, but after graduation he refused to work at the Centre. He wanted to go to college and major in Management. It was one of two courses available now. College graduates supervised factories or stores or the Centre, saving up until they could afford a virtual life. Some of them became teachers, who made slightly less than supervisors, but occupied an exalted place in society and were assured of a virtual life upon retirement, paid for by the government. But college was expensive and they couldn't afford to send him. Nick didn't have any money to invest in the world stock market either so he bummed around for a couple of years, much to their dad's disappointment. Then their father had become ill, and as the treatment for cancer was expensive, Nick reluctantly joined Delia at the Centre so he could help out.

Delia was getting hungry just watching Art eat, so she reached into the small food locker underneath his chair for part of her daily ration. It was the apprentices' job to stock the food lockers each day and the rest of the time to attend lectures and to observe the live action videos of the caretakers at work.

After Art ate, he talked to an imaginary girlfriend on the phone. Delia knew from his profile that he had never found the perfect girl for him while he was living in the real world. Nobody understood him, he complained in his essay. Sure, he was popular, but the people who lived with him always told him he took things too seriously and laughed at things that were important to him. By the time he chose to go virtual, his popularity was flagging. He wasn't as young as he used to be and he was afraid his imagination and energy were waning.

How Delia wished she had known him before he had gone virtual. She would have understood him, she was sure, and could have been a friend to him. Maybe he would have found the perfect girl in her. She wondered what his virtual girlfriend was like.

Then Art went to the park, apparently to meet his girlfriend. Lucky him. There hadn't been green grass and trees in Manila since her high school graduation, except at the grounds of the Cultural Centre of the Philippines Museum, which could only be accessed by robots and seen from the windows of the Virtual Centre. Parks were low priority by now anyway, since most people were too busy working at the Centre all day. The middle class, the supervisors, had their own homes in the distant suburbs with grass and trees and flowers. They monitored the factories, farms, stores, national security, power plants, museums, and the Centre by computer, and they had cooperative stores in their neighbourhoods so they need never go to the dirty city. Teachers came from the suburbs also and had their own shuttle to take them to their assigned schools. But luckily the school was air-conditioned. Delia's house was near the edge of the enormous landfill and it depressed her terribly to return there every day after working at the sterile Centre. But housing was hard to find these days and that was the best place they could afford.

She wouldn't mind leading a virtual life herself, she thought. In her virtual world, she would live in the beautiful green suburbs. She would have a garden filled with every flower in existence. She would be married to Reggie, whom she had never forgotten. They would have two or three children. They'd have all the modern appliances, and spend their days playing outdoors and listening to music. They could even travel. Nobody left the country nowadays. It wasn't necessary since for business there was e-mail and there was virtual travel for those who just wanted a vacation. It was much cheaper. Delia had tried it once when she got her Christmas bonus. But, of course, one thing the computer couldn't recreate was Reggie and the experience of having him by her side. After a while, it got boring swimming at the virgin beach alone. But if she described him accurately, she would be able to have him back in her virtual world.

The rest of the day went as usual. Mariel's DOM made startlingly loud grunting noises and soothed a jealous girlfriend who had apparently caught him in the act. The new apprentice nearly fell asleep while the politician made a lengthy speech. Bert's old woman was thrilled to receive the news that she was going to be a grandmother. Her other neighbour's old woman prayed a novena. The ex-movie star on Mariel's other side amused them by going ballroom dancing, swinging her arms, kicking her legs, and swaying in her seat. Art spent a lot of his time singing.

Finally, the last bell rang and everyone yawned and stretched and stood up to go. Delia joined the tide of workers going to the MRT station. Many of her friends stopped her to chat but she apologized, telling them she was too tired, and hurried to the turnstile. Delia thought she saw Nick in the crowd but she told herself she was hallucinating. She didn't know where he'd gone but he was probably leading a demonstration in Malacañang, which was now maintained as a museum only. People often held symbolic demonstrations there anyway, knowing that the security cameras would show their activities to the government officials in their homes in the suburbs.

She reached into her pocket for her wallet. It wasn't there. She looked for it on the floor. Could it have fallen? Nobody stole wallets these days, as you couldn't access money in people's bank accounts and debit card machines demanded a thumbprint before acknowledging the transfer of cash. There was an impatient line forming behind her and she apologized as she retraced her steps. Where was the wallet? She went all the way back to Art's place. The apprentices were there cleaning up and restocking the food lockers. Her wallet was on the floor under her chair. Most of the apprentices had finished their work by then and were leaving. She should leave too. But she paused to gaze at Art, who was smiling and whispering, 'I love you.' To his girlfriend, Delia supposed. He looked so happy and Delia longed to experience what he was experiencing. She impulsively bent and kissed him, and he continued to smile.

The door alarm was sounding. The last remaining apprentices hurried through and Delia ran after them. But just as she reached the door, there was an ear-splitting explosion. The door slammed shut before she could go through and she crouched against it instinctively, covering her head. She felt the rush of the stinking air and the sprinkling of pulverized glass as the windows shattered. Alarms were going off all over the place, and she heard the sound of screams and stampeding feet down the moving walk.

A rope was dropped through one window, and someone carrying a bright emergency lamp slid down it. Nick, of course.

'What have you done?' she screamed at him.

He looked at her with concern. 'No, I can't believe I set off the bombs too early. My fault for being too excited. Are you all right, Del?' He went to her and held out his hand. She leaped to her feet without his aid. 'Guess you're all right,' he said. He put down the emergency lamp and went to the bodies, pulling off electrodes and undoing straps.

'What are you doing?' Delia demanded. 'Explain! The authorities will be here soon, and I'd like to know what to tell them.'

'Oh, don't worry about them. They think the door has safely trapped me here until they're finished attending to the hysterical people outside. The security system didn't take into account someone blasting off the glass with homemade bombs and climbing through on a rope anchored to the steel with an electromagnet, also homemade, and pretty strong. Another fault of our government.'

'Some of these people could die,' Delia told him. 'That lady, the one who's always praying, must be over a hundred years old.'

'Okay, I'll concentrate my energies on the younger ones. Like this guy.' He yanked the food tube out of Art's nose.

'But why?' Delia asked.

'They're the ones who've entrapped us in our lives, Delia,' Nick exclaimed. 'Because of them, we've lost our freedom to choose how we'll make a living. Our entire lives centre around taking care of the rich so their money will take care of us.'

'What's wrong with that?' Delia said. 'It seems like a fair arrangement to me. I was always happy with it.'

'Are you happy that they control the government, that they made the rules before they went out like this and we continue to follow them like programmed robots? We're kept so busy by their demands that we've even stopped noticing what an unhealthy place the real world is becoming.'

'So what? Someday we could go virtual too.'

'If everyone were living in a virtual world, who would keep people alive?' Nick yanked off the last of the electrodes on Art and started working on his straps. 'They've set up the system in such a way that we can't ever get out, so we'll always be there to look after them. Why do you think higher education is so expensive? So the lower classes won't learn how to operate supercomputers and complex machines. And we can't sabotage them either. And, of course, we are taught by our middle-class teachers who have been bribed by the promise of an eternal virtual life after retirement that the system is perfect. Perfect for these people maybe, but not for us.' He removed Art's mask and gave his shoulder a shake. 'Come on, buddy, it's time to see what's happened to the real world since you've gone.' Art rolled over and fell on the floor. 'Ow!' he yelled, and sat up and rubbed his eyes. Nick went on to free the politician while Delia knelt at Art's side. 'Don't be scared,' she said.

Art was looking around him in puzzlement. 'What is this, a morgue?' he asked.

'It's a ward for people who . . . just want to rest.' Delia didn't know if she should explain. 'Art, do you feel okay?' she asked.

'I'm starving!'

She pointed to her food locker. 'There's food there, help yourself. Though you'll be back soon.' He helped himself to a sandwich, unwrapped it and took a big bite, then took a swig from her water jug.

The politician, now freed, stood up and reached his hand out to Art. 'Thank you for voting for me,' he said. Art shook his hand, still looking puzzled, and suddenly the politician clutched at his chest and crumpled to the floor. Delia rushed to him and put her ear to his chest, then began CPR. 'He must have gotten a heart attack from the shock,' she told Nick. 'Nick, please stop. The shock is going to be too much, they'll just die and you won't accomplish anything!'

Nick ignored her and unstrapped the former movie star. She mumbled, 'I need my beauty sleep,' and covered her face with her arm. Nick went on to a fat Chinese man.

Delia just kept on doing CPR. There was a heartbeat, and she leaned back with relief against the politician's chair. She looked at Art. He took out a bag of chips and opened it as he gobbled up the rest of his sandwich. He looked at her, swallowed and apologized, 'Such manners, I know, but somehow food never tasted this good. Thanks, miss. What's your name?'

'Delia. I already know you're Art Layag.'

'Do I know you?' he asked.

'I'm a fan.' It was true enough and she felt the truth was too complicated to explain now.

'Don't lie to them!' Nick exploded. 'How can I accomplish my purpose if they don't know the truth?' He ripped the mask off the Chinese man, who sat up and blinked. Nick started working on another person. 'What's the last thing you remember, Art?

Art smiled. 'Sleeping with my girlfriend.'

'No, before that, way back. Do the words "virtual life" mean anything to you?'

Art thought for a while. 'That rings a bell.' He paused, then said, 'I remember signing these papers. I wanted a certain kind of life and they promised it to me. They promised I would never get old or die. I would be free to do whatever I wanted.'

'Free!' Nick laughed. 'That's a good one. Only in your mind.'

'Well, what other kind of freedom is there?' asked Art.

'The old-fashioned kind,' Nick said. 'The kind of freedom which you don't obtain at the expense of half of society's freedom. The kind of freedom where you are free to act but not to choose the outcome of your actions. That is freedom!'

'Well, I was happy the way things were,' Art said. 'I miss my girlfriend.'

There was a soft whir and Delia looked up to see a government security helicopter approaching.

'They're after me,' Nick said calmly. 'Listen, Delia, I'll tell them you weren't involved. They'll probably let you out through the door. But you'd better escape through the emergency entrance once it's unlocked and bring whoever's awake and alive with you. Bring them to our house. That ought to be enough.'

'They don't have cards for the turnstile,' Delia pointed out.

'Take them for a walk along the Bay, then.' The helicopter was fast approaching and a long, thin robot arm shot out and snapped up Nick. 'Do it for me!' he ordered Delia, as he rose through the air.

She didn't say anything. She wasn't going to do what he said. She didn't care if the security cameras were probably all damaged in the explosion. She had never been a rebel and she wasn't about to start now. She would see to it herself that everyone was reinstalled in his or her virtual world.

Art was looking at her now. 'Are you really a fan? I'd like to get to know you.'

'What about your girlfriend?' she said teasingly.

'Just because I have a girlfriend doesn't mean I can't talk to other girls.'

'Well, she wasn't real anyway.'

He frowned deeply. 'Are you sure?'

Delia was worried that he no longer remembered which parts of his life were real and which were manufactured. 'Maybe it would be better if you went back,' she said. 'If you want to. I don't think I can, though. I don't think they'll allow me to take care of you anymore.'

'Take care of me? Why would you need to? I can look after myself.'

'I suppose. It's just I looked after you all these years—'

'Like I was a child?' He seemed offended. 'Hey, I don't need a mother.'

'Do you miss your mom?' she asked suddenly, remembering the pain of her own loss.

'Nanay is alive and well. She lives in the mountains in a home with a beautiful view and I go visit her when I want to chill. She's always excited to hear my new songs and she and my girlfriend get along great . . .'

Then he stopped. 'You said my girlfriend wasn't real. And I'm getting the sense that—'

'Yes, in real life your mother died.' She touched his arm. 'I know it's hard to take. Is that why you went virtual? You were rich and famous and had a wonderful life, so I always wondered why—'

'I never thought about it before but I guess it was. I know I seemed to have a good life, but it was empty. I loved what I was doing, but I couldn't share my joy and success with the one person who'd mattered to me. And there was nobody else. I'd come to believe I could never find anyone I could relax and be real with.'

'But you were happy in your virtual life, weren't you? I made sure of it, reading about you, observing what you enjoyed—'

'Right. That was your job.'

'A job I loved to do.' He looked at her intently, and she looked down, feeling herself blush. He went on, 'I was happy and yet, I didn't feel I was in control of my life. Maybe I don't need to go back to that. Maybe all I need is someone like you. Someone really real, who knows me.'

Tremulously, she said, 'I'm not sure you can just walk away. They receive payments from your account while you're in that state. They might not want to let you go.'

'Who are "they"? Whoever they are, I'm not afraid of them. Nobody takes my freedom away from me,' Art declared. He picked up a large package of cookies. 'I don't really know what's going on, if there was a bomb or anything but we'd better have provisions if we're going into hiding.' He handed her the package, filled his arms with sandwiches and hooked the handle of the jug of water with one finger.

A click informed Delia that the door was now unlocked. As it rose slowly to reveal the feet of the Centre's supervisors, she made her decision. She picked up the emergency lamp, tucked the package of cookies under her arm, grabbed Art's elbow and hurried to the emergency exit opposite. She turned the handle, and, ignoring the door alarm, went through, followed by Art.

She didn't know where they were going exactly. She was surprised to find herself on the edge of the bay, on the grounds of the Cultural Centre. She hadn't been there since she was a little girl. Nobody really bothered going to the museums, except students. They had been to all the museums for school trips but there was never anything new in them, so what was the point of going more than once or twice?

She crouched behind the wall, and Art followed suit. Delia wondered if they should run, but she did not see anyone at the emergency exit. They must be too preoccupied with the bodies to bother with her, she thought. Or maybe they believed that since Nick had been captured, they had nothing left to worry about. Another flaw in their government, Nick would say.

Art tensed at first, looked around wildly, then took a chance and peeked over the wall. 'I guess we're safe,' he said. Delia looked too. The emergency door was shut, though they hadn't bothered to close it. It must have shut automatically, or maybe one of the Centre's officials closed it.

Art stood on the edge of the wall and looked about him. 'Things have changed a lot in just a short time. Where are all the boats?'

'You've been asleep for twelve years,' Delia told him. 'Boats have been phased out. No more international trade, no more need to travel outside of the country. There are MRT systems to take us to the cities and suburbs.'

'Progress comes with a price,' Art said. 'Did you know that I practically grew up here? My mother and I lived on the grounds of the Cultural Centre. She begged to put food in our mouths. She died suddenly when I was about eleven and I was found by the authorities and placed in an orphan's home. That was where my singing talent was discovered, and the rest is history.' Art sat down on the wall. 'I remember swimming here, and fishing, too. We didn't really catch much.'

'Just as well since a lot of the fish were poisoned,' Delia told him.

'I liked watching the boats best, though, and sometimes I would dream of stowing away on one of them and seeing the world.'

'Nowadays, all you need to do is go to a virtual travel salon,' Delia told him.

'I didn't think that would really catch on, virtual travel. That's just like looking through a guidebook! You don't really get to experience a place, do you? You see things, but nothing happens to you. No adventure!' Art said. He turned to look at the dying palms. 'I used to climb those and bring down coconuts.' And he laughed. 'I sound like an old man, yearning for the good old days.'

'You're almost forty, you know,' Delia informed him. 'I'm ten years younger than you, I'm twenty-nine.'

Art looked down at himself in shock. He peered at his bony hands, inspected his long, grey-streaked hair. 'My God,' he gasped. 'No wonder the world has changed so much.'

'Those boats you talk about, they're in museums now,' Delia told him. 'There's a naval museum down there.' She pointed to the other end of the bay, where there was an enormous tent and a few ships chained together. 'Come on, let's go there.' Art followed her like an obedient child.

Museums were never closed, though all the objects were kept safe from prying hands all day and night with burglar alarms. But there weren't really any objects displayed on the ships, anyway. They were the display themselves.

'I wish we could sail this ship,' Art said, as they walked along the deck of an early twentieth-century model.

'Where would we go?' asked Delia, dreamily.

'Aren't there still uninhabited islands around here?' Art asked.

'Lots.'

'Maybe we could live on one of them. Like those people in that show they used to have when I was a kid, *Survivor*. Did you ever watch that? They were always showing the reruns.'

'I don't think I remember seeing that,' Delia said. 'When I was a kid, technology was all anyone was interested in. Virtuality, especially.'

'I can't believe I bought into that,' Art said.

'But you were happy enough.'

'I thought I was,' Art said darkly. 'I guess I was, but I always felt there was something missing, and now, after our great escape, I know what it was.'

'What?' Delia still didn't understand what could have been missing.

'Adventure,' Art said. 'Challenge, surprise.'

'You sometimes got frustrated over your music,' Delia told him.

'Petty, very petty of me,' Art said. 'Here I am, nearly forty and I haven't grown as a person at all. In my virtual world, I was always twenty-seven or so. I never grew older and I faced the same type of petty challenges over and over. I think I'd like to try something new.' He tossed the things he was carrying in a lifeboat and inspected the pulleys that held it in place. Amidst horrible squeaking, he managed to let the boat down a little way, just until it was level with the deck.

Delia expected an alarm to go off somewhere, but there was no sound other than that unbearable screech of the rusted pulleys. 'You know,' Art said. 'I could use your help, Delia.'

'I don't know how these things work,' she said, nervously.

'Not that. I can figure out the mechanism. There's a sail here; I'm sure I can figure out how to set that up too. It's you I want, Delia. I need you to face the challenge of starting a new life with me. Will you come?' He held out his hand.

Delia shuddered. 'We only have a few provisions. We could die out there.'

'We can get some more. Let's take things as they come. That's how my mother and I did it, and I survived.'

She gazed at the face of the man she had cared for the past twelve years. She noted the determination in his expression. And she knew she could not leave him to risk his life alone, no matter how foolhardy she thought his enterprise was. She took his hand and climbed into the boat.

After much creaking, they hit the water. Art then struggled with the mast. Finally, he unfurled the sail. They rode with a strong breeze to the south, not thinking to steer.

They rationed their food and water carefully. Just when they thought they were going to succumb to dehydration, Art sighted an island. He took an oar and rowed them closer, struggling against the wind, then decided to adjust the sail. The boat drifted onto the shore of the tiny island.

Art was at first disappointed to see some crumbling houses. Then he realized that they were abandoned.

There was a grove of coconut trees behind the houses. Art scrambled up one, laughing like a boy, and tossed a bunch of coconuts to the ground. He battered one against a sharp stone until it split open. He handed the shell to Delia, and they ate their first meal on their very own island. That was how they began their new life together.

It was a wonderful life but sometimes Delia wondered if they were really better off. She longed for her father and brother. Before she disconnected her device, she received a news report that Nick had been captured. In the video, he seemed to be revelling in recounting to the government all their ills and seemed to be facing the challenge of arguing for himself in his pending trial with glee.

She prayed he would go free. She lived in a constant state of anxiety, wondering how he was, and her father hooked up to hospital machines like those in the Centre, but without the virtual comforts Art and the others like him had received. She feared to give birth to her first child alone. She was bored a great deal, much more than Art, who was having fun trying out the musical instruments he made from odds and ends.

She filled her lonely hours when Art was busy improvising songs with wondering. And waiting. The child grew within her. And her fear grew, not fear of the pain of childbirth, but fear that she was somehow cheating the child of a better life by remaining here with Art. He was loving towards her, he was determined to be a good father, but surely the child needed more than that. She had to provide the child with all the available advantages, didn't she? Any good mother would want her child to have the best life possible. She wondered what world her children would choose. Would they go back to the polluted cities and work as caretakers at the Centre? Certainly they couldn't go to college. Would they remain here and farm to stay alive? But how could they be content and happy knowing there was a world of wonders across the waves that they had never experienced? She sat on the beach for long hours, staring in the direction of Manila and wondering, 'What was the best way to live?' She could not decide.

2

Hatchling

The vast night sky sparkled with a multitude of stars, each enticing with its possibilities. But the young man walking beneath it in the sleepy town was not one to entertain possibilities of other worlds with intelligent beings. In any case, his gaze was set not toward the sky but toward the house of an old classmate up a hill.

Jacob paused to see if the lights were still burning in Sofia's house before he proceeded up the hillside. Provincial folk kept early hours. He was just from the city, a boarder at the science high school home for his summer vacation.

Sofia should have been with him. Through all their years together in their small-town school, she had won as many honours as he had and had been his only serious rival in science and maths quiz bees. It had riled him back then, but now he felt sorry for her. She was all set to go with him. Like him, she had received a government scholarship to the most prestigious science high school. But her family, at the last minute, pressured her against going. There was a new baby expected, and they needed her around to help.

He supposed her younger brothers couldn't be expected to be of much help with a baby—if anything, they'd only cause more trouble, but he didn't see why her older sister wouldn't be enough help. She couldn't earn that much as a waitress; she might as well let her younger sister who had a shot at a much brighter future have a chance. Even if it meant having to work less hours. Whereas if she'd had her shot at a better education, bright and hardworking Sofia would be sure to get into a good college later and land a brilliant job and uplift the status of her entire family. It infuriated Jacob that he could have worked this out at fourteen and Sofia's family couldn't.

But that was how things went. Now Jacob was wondering how things had gone with her after one year. After spending his first day home with his family, who hadn't changed a bit since he left, he decided to go and see her.

He hadn't gloated when he learned she was staying in their backward town. He was competitive, but not mean. He had sent a sympathetic message and that led to a friendly chat, the first of many. He wished he had not wasted all those years trying to outstrip her instead of getting to know her.

He hadn't even known her house was like this—a ramshackle wooden structure with flaking greyish-white paint, and little boys running and yelling in the yard with a dog. There was the piercing scream of a baby, then a young woman appeared at an upstairs window holding a bundled-up infant. She stuck out her head and called down to the boys, 'Can you keep it down? I'm trying to get the baby to sleep.'

Then her eye fell on Jacob. 'What are you doing here?' Sofia demanded.

To be heard, he'd have to yell over the din that still hadn't subsided. He imagined himself shouting up to her, 'I came to see you.' It seemed too much like a modern rom-com version of Romeo and Juliet, so he just smiled, waved, and gestured to her to come down. She nodded but gestured toward the baby. He nodded back, then went to join Sofia's brothers in the yard. He gamely played soccer with them for a bit. When the sound of crying stopped, he glanced towards the door, but it didn't open, so he continued to play with the boys until Sofia suddenly stepped out, carrying a plate of sliced pineapple.

'You boys should be getting ready for bed. Not you, Jacob.'

'It's summer,' one protested.

'Too hot inside to sleep,' whined another.

The third brother simply ignored her and started kicking the ball again. She stepped down from the porch and put one foot down on it. The boys groaned and went inside. 'Good night,' Sofia said sweetly. 'And don't bother the baby.'

As the screen door slammed behind the last little boy, she shook her head. 'It's hard to believe that they were such cute babies once.'

'You seem to know how to handle them,' he remarked.

She smiled at him, handed him the plate of fruit, then plunked herself down on the porch steps. After a moment, Jacob awkwardly sat down beside her. This wasn't the way they did things at his house. They would have invited a guest in, or if they wanted to stay on the porch, they had a few rattan chairs there for the purpose. Certainly in the summer it was cooler outside, a better place to receive visitors, but to ask them to sit on dusty steps didn't seem quite right.

Of course, he was just an old school friend. He had to admit that it wasn't really the lack of furniture that made him feel awkward sitting there. It was sitting beside a girl all alone in the sudden silence. When they were fourteen, it wouldn't have been such a big deal. Somehow it felt different now that they were fifteen. She seemed different in a way he couldn't quite say. Softer and curvier, sort of. He didn't want to think about it too much. It embarrassed him.

He felt he had to say something, so he said the first thing that came to mind. 'How are your sister and the baby?'

There were few secrets in a town their size, and Jacob had already heard that the new baby wasn't her mother's, but her older sister, Janet's. Janet worked as a waitress at what passed for a resort at their beach. Theirs was a beach town but far from a glamorous one, with its gritty grey volcanic sand. The local kids didn't care and would go play along the surf every day. Once you reached your teens, though, you were sophisticated enough to realize how unglamorous and unkempt this bit of shore was and stayed away unless you were an avid swimmer or wanted some time with a special someone.

He supposed they had tried to hide the facts, but how could they in this little town? He had already heard all about Janet's baby out of wedlock, how white he was, with strange slanted eyes. Some said it was a mongoloid, others insisted its father was a Korean tourist passing through town on one of those budget tours. Their town was itself not a tourist attraction, but it was sometimes used by tour companies as a stopover for a cheap but excellent seafood meal. As awful as the beach was, with grainy dark sand, for a certain type of tourist it had its attraction—a few huts whose owners hawked them to couples for 'short-time'. Jacob had seen Janet parading the beach in skimpy tops. He could well imagine how the baby came into being.

Sofia told him as she led him out to the porch, 'The baby is huge and doesn't look like anyone in the family in the least. He's too fair and has fine black hair.' She twisted one of her thick black curls around her finger as she offered him the plate of pineapple.

'Sure it's not a changeling?'

Sofia laughed shortly and took a piece of pineapple herself. She always seemed to get his jokes whereas his other friends usually looked at him as if he was demented when he kidded around. She licked juice delicately from her fingers.

'He's really cute. When he's not crying, that is.'

He figured that meant he cried a lot.

'Janet took a night shift to help pay for his formula and stuff. Dad expects her to. So I have to look after him as soon as I get home from school. I'm best with him, anyway.' She smiled proudly, but with a hint of weariness and resignation, which suggested to him that the care of the baby fell mainly upon her.

He looked at her. 'You know, it's bad enough that they kept you from going to high school in the city. You shouldn't be forced to take so much responsibility for a baby that isn't even yours.'

'What can I do when his mom can't take care of him?'

'She'll do it if she has to!' he said forcefully. 'It's instinct, isn't it? All species have the instinct to nurture their young. If they don't, they'd become extinct.'

'Without that instinct, they'd become extinct?' She smiled. 'But what about all the species that don't take care of their young? Fish, insects, reptiles. Except that dinosaur, the maiasaur, wasn't it? Didn't they look after their babies? You're the one with an obsession with dinosaurs.'

'Only till I was in third grade!' he protested, flushing. 'But that one species is an exception. Maybe if the dinos took care of their young better, they would have remained the kings of the world. But, you know, they were reptiles. Which don't exactly go around carrying their babies on their back.'

'Any more than bugs do,' she said, brushing tiny moths away from her face. She blinked, and Jacob noticed for the first time the dark curling lashes that framed her wide, intelligent eyes. He'd never really thought much about girls, finding most of them silly, but this girl had something about her. At least she was interesting to talk to.

What was she saying now? 'You know, except for the dinosaurs, they seem to be doing pretty well.' She slapped at a mosquito and showed him the squashed insect on her palm as if to prove a point. But what point she was trying to make wasn't really clear to him.

'What are you saying?' he said. 'That a species doesn't need an instinct to take care of babies to survive?'

'Kind of. And even if there is, some individuals might not have it. I don't think it would be fair for a poor little baby to suffer just because his mother happens to be one of those. That's probably why we stick with our families, anyway. Would you be where you are today if it weren't for your family?'

He flushed defensively. His parents were well-known among the kids as the ones who shooed away everyone who came calling him to play every day but Saturday. And even then, he was often busy with some kind of lesson or project.

'I'm not making fun of you,' she added quickly. 'I think you were lucky. You got into that school, didn't you?'

'So did you,' he pointed out.

'Oh, well, but I'm a nerd by nature. I actually like studying even if nobody makes me. It's the one way to get people to leave you in peace in a home with five kids.'

It occurred to him that if she had been able to get the grades she did with no help and encouragement from her family, it must mean that she was also a natural genius. Probably smarter than him. The thought riled him.

'So, now that you gave up your one chance to get a good high school education, what's going to happen to you? You'll probably end up a statistic, just another Filipina nurse or caregiver.'

'I don't plan to be, but even if that does happen, what's so bad about it? You get paid a decent wage and you get to help others.'

'Help others!' he snorted. 'What about helping yourself? You know, you girls always complain about how you're the underdogs, that guys get all the opportunities just because we're guys. But maybe you just lose out because you're scared to fight for what you really want. You could tell your family off. Force your sister to look after her own baby, make your brothers help, but you don't.'

'You may find this hard to believe, but it's my choice,' she shot back. 'A choice I made because I care about my family. It's not like I've dropped out of high school. I'm still working hard to get into a good college.'

'What for, when they might not even let you go?' he muttered.

She glanced over her shoulder, placed the empty plate down on the porch step, and rose to her feet. She walked out to the street, and he drifted along with her.

'I don't mean to insult your parents, but it just seems unfair. And it-it *infuriates* me that you don't seem to be bothered by it. I don't understand it!'

'Why should you?' she said with a quizzical smile.

'Why should I care?' Now that he thought about it, he couldn't understand why either. Of course, he cared about things being right and fair, but why he cared about it to the degree he did, he couldn't quite say.

'Actually, I meant, why should you understand? Or rather, how can you? I've heard your sisters complain. They have chores and tasks at home but you get away with doing practically nothing. And your mother is known for always bragging about you, doing anything for you, even if she is strict with you. And maybe you're not rich, but your family has never struggled to make ends meet like mine has. You couldn't possibly understand what it's like to feel obligated to help your family.'

He opened his mouth to argue but suddenly they were both transfixed as a bright light streaked across the sky and flared into a wide halo of light in the valley below.

'Was that a meteorite?' Sofia asked.

'Could be,' Jacob said, nervously nibbling once more at the pineapple wedge he still held in his hand, though nothing was left but the hard, fibrous rib. 'I've never seen one myself.'

'Let's go see.' Sofia took the rib from him and tossed it in the bushes, then she grabbed his hand, still sticky with juice.

They dashed down the hill, winding their way past the long line of trees they had played among in childhood. Too mesmerized by her goal to see menace in the tall, encroaching dark shapes, she merely pointed at a ribbon of smoky vapour rising from behind the trees.

'I hope it didn't start a forest fire,' Jacob muttered. He didn't really think it was safe to be blundering through the woods in the dark, even in their sleepy town. He had never believed in creatures of the night that all provincial folk seemed to—hairy giants that lurked in the trees, vampiric female beings, the carnivorous *tiyanak* that took the form of a tiny child. Still, you never knew who or what might be lurking in the dark. But he could hardly leave Sofia, who was intent on finding the meteorite, and whose hand now seemed fused to his.

They continued to make their way through the sparse woods towards the direction of the smoke. Eventually, he could see nothing that hinted at the presence of a meteorite. Jacob was about to suggest that they turn back when there was a flash of gold, and a brilliant path of light spread before them.

'Look,' Sofia breathed.

A large black pod, visible only in the darkness by its faint sheen, hovered slightly above the ground. The light was streaming through its open door, from which stepped down a reptilian creature bearing a white ovoid form in its arms. Jacob pulled Sofia back into the shadows as the creature moved toward their direction. Despite its scaly body and its thin black tongue that flicked in and out, there was a human-like aspect to its appearance. The creature was the size of a very tall man, thanks mainly to its long arching neck, and its beady eyes set on each side of its head, just above its rounded snout, reflected a definite spark of intelligence as it surveyed its surroundings, and it walked upright, clothed in a short tunic from which protruded the end of a pointy tail.

The lizard-like creature did not go far. It lay its bundle down under a tree then, grunting, it raised its claw-like hand and gave the ovoid one fierce slash with a lethal two-inch nail. Having done so, it turned and climbed back into its hovering craft. The stream of light abruptly disappeared as the door slid shut.

They could barely discern the black craft flying off, could hear nothing. For some minutes they watched after it as well as they could, straining their eyes to see what path it was taking through the sky. Then they heard a whimpering cry. Sofia's eyes snapped to the ground. Instinctively she approached the white bundle under the tree, from which the cry was issuing.

The white case had settled into leathery folds, looking in the darkness like a smooth blanket swaddling an infant. A round face now poked out, its features barely visible in the darkness. But its cry drew Sofia and she stepped toward the creature, reaching for it.

'No!' Jacob leaped forward to grab her and pull her away—just as the creature's face stretched forward on its long reptilian neck, its razor teeth bared and its long black tongue lashing out in ravenous greed. He pulled Sofia along with him through the trees, up the hill, until she cried out and collapsed against him. He stared down at her in horror, but she was merely gasping for breath, clutching her ribcage, so he gently seated her on a large protruding tree root, all the while watching to see if the alien creature had followed. Thankfully, it had not.

As soon as Sofia had enough breath back in her she sputtered, 'That creature—it was like a *tiyanak*, wasn't it?'

'Uh-huh.'

'What was all that? What did it mean?'

He stood silent, leaning on the trunk of the tree as he tried to form his thoughts.

The idea that came to him was this: Perhaps on another planet, a parallel world, dinosaurs had remained the dominant creature, had survived and evolved into intelligent beings. But with their natural aversion to caring for young, they had devised systems to protect their offspring, one of which was taking hatching eggs out to various parts of the planet dominated by nurturing humans and leaving the hatchlings there to grow, unthreatened by predators or competitors. Perhaps they chose the Philippines particularly for its tender-hearted people who would find it difficult to resist an infant's cry and thus be lured to become the hatchling's prey. He couldn't recall hearing of a similar folk belief in any other country. And he supposed that once they had grown large enough, fattened on human meat, and strong enough to fend for themselves the creatures would be taken back to their reptilian planet.

Shakily, he slid down the trunk and reached out to Sofia to soothe her and maybe find comfort himself, as he gave his explanation. But just as he sat down she jumped to her feet, terror and fatigue forgotten, her face turned uphill towards her house. 'The baby!' she said.

Now that she mentioned it, he could hear the infant's cry coming faintly, soon followed by the impetuous wail of the irritated young mother now home from work.

'I'm coming,' Sofia called out to her family who could not hear her.

'Why?' Jacob protested. 'It's not your baby. You don't have to—' But she ignored him and hurried up the hill. Jacob rose slowly, in a state of irritation. Why did she care so much, to the point of sacrificing herself, her future? Though when he thought about it, why did he care? He supposed he saw her in a different way from her family, who were all too absorbed in their own concerns to note her performance in school. But that didn't explain why he cared about someone who he should've been glad to have trounced. Well, someone had to care, look after her interests since, exasperatingly, she wouldn't do it herself.

She was far ahead now despite the darkness of the path. He quickened his pace to catch up with her, with just one last swift glance over his shoulder down the hill, where the creature of horror still lay.

3

The Creator Defends his Creation

How do I plead? Well, Your Honour, let us make this short and simple, something no political trial in our country has ever been in the last hundred years or more. And, for a change, you'll get your man with absolute proof. Guilty beyond reasonable doubt, as they say. Yes, I plead guilty. But I do not apologize.

I am, of course, aware that I committed fraud. Indirectly, perhaps. I built the robot and programmed him. But I never tried to pass off my android as human. I simply let people think he was. All right, perhaps that kind of concealment is fraud. But I never told anyone to nominate or elect him for president. The people chose him and since we are supposed to have a democracy here, then shouldn't we accept the people's vote? Oh, yes, the constitution does state that the president must be a person, a natural-born Filipino citizen and all that. But this robot is a person, if you mean by a person someone with his own identity (the constitutional definition needs updating, don't you think?), and he was indeed born here. At least, I made him here.

No, Your Honour, I didn't intend to make a mockery of these proceedings. I apologize if what I said seemed offensive or inappropriate. But I still do not apologize for my act.

Look at the presidents we've had the past hundred years. Mostly incompetent. The better ones were too fearful of public opinion to really do any good. Because, let's face it, elections here are just a popularity contest. There are plenty of good intelligent people in our country who could do a good job as president. But nobody would vote for them. Take me as an example. Now, I don't think I'd make a truly great president but I could do a much better job than a lot of people who actually were elected to that office. I've had more schooling than most presidents, I think. I have a Ph.D. I've worked on many scientific projects all over the world. I've written books about science. I don't know how many people here have read them—probably not many or they would have caught my hint in my last book. I have it here, Your Honour. I wrote quite plainly that, 'Robots may do a better job of running the world than people, if they are programmed by a select group of intelligent and virtuous individuals.' In a perfect world, everyone would agree who would be the best individuals to accomplish this task. But this isn't a perfect world, Your Honour. I know I'm not perfect. So I based my robot's program on the beliefs of certain great thinkers, which are also my basis for my personal value system.

What I couldn't do by myself was make him charismatic. Obviously, I'm not like that or I could have gotten myself elected as president myself. People have branded me a nerd ever since I started school, and while true, that didn't exactly win me respect. Being interested in learning never seems to, these days.

To make him attractive to people and good at dealing with them, I observed and interviewed my uncle, a leader of a charismatic group, and my wife, a psychologist. I programmed my creation's personality then according to their suggestions. For the record, they had no idea what I really intended to do: to create a well-programmed robot to run this country.

I saw my opportunity to attract attention to him in the last People Power Revolution. I got him to inspire the EDSA 9 crowd with speeches. It certainly worked. In fact, it worked beyond my wildest dreams! Everyone noticed him, everyone was soon asking about him, looking for him, trying to find out who he was. It helped that I made him good-looking. But, more than that, his way of showing concern for people moved all those he met. He never forgot a face or a name. He remembered everything about the people he met—their hopes, their worries. Everything. And he really did something to help each one, however small a gesture. Though could any of his gestures really be said to be small? He charmed big businessmen into sponsoring poor children. He single-handedly hammered roofs onto storm-damaged houses. And everywhere cameras were following him. Reporters hounded him.

I hardly expected that he would be elected president so soon. But that sad business with the last president and vice-president dragged on so long, new proofs of each one's corruption constantly being uncovered till nobody was too enthusiastic about putting either in the position of president.

Personally, I was always amazed that anyone had voted for them in the first place. I wouldn't have.

Well, the president knew how to get attention, I'll give him that, shocking with his crude wit. The promises he made were nothing new. Perhaps his irreverence and daring gave the impression to the people he'd have the courage to wipe out crime and corruption. The vice president was a contrast to him, cool and dignified, from a traditional political family. They were an odd pair running together but I suppose they balanced each other out. The VP seemed all right to me, at first. But when the president's corruption was exposed, she went from fully supporting him to declaring she knew nothing about his actions and turning against him entirely, only to do the exact same things he'd done once she was settled in his position.

The next thing I knew, she was being charged and impeached as well, then there was a revolution of the disillusioned masses grown impatient with the legal proceedings, and my android was thrust into their place.

Now you cannot deny that he did a good job, Your Honour. Was any president more tireless? He worked efficiently all day long. Even when he was supposed to be sleeping he really was working—I was programming new information into his brain. I have to say I am surprised that people did not notice that he never ate or slept until some talk-show host decided to do an exposé on how he achieved his legendary tirelessness and almost superhuman strength.

Was any president braver? He went everywhere without bodyguards, even to war-torn regions. So impressed were people with his courage, as well as his sincere speeches and sensible proposals, that we finally have peace throughout the land for the first time since . . . I don't know when. Maybe right after World War II. And that's almost a hundred and fifty years ago!

Yes, of course, he's a machine. So he can't really feel any emotion. Is that so much of a disadvantage? Emotion often clouds the mind. Yes, it sometimes inspires good but so can being observant and logical.

And, all right, maybe he isn't really a person. He isn't an individual, exactly, since I've programmed into him all that I see is best in myself and my wife, uncle, and other friends and relatives, and all the great thinkers whose works I've read. So he's not a genetic accident, a random hodgepodge of often conflicting personality traits we human beings are. But that's why he always makes so much sense! Not just from my point of view, but others'.

To tell the truth, Your Honour, I don't really want an android to run this country. I want a human being to do it, a natural-born citizen we can be proud of. Someone who is truly representative of all that's best in our people. There are people like that, I think, or at least who come close. But until one of them gets elected as president, I think we should let my creation govern.

Yes, you have a point, Your Honour, in saying that I'm really the one running the country through this robot. But wasn't it that way with most of our presidents? They had their backers and advisers. They had so many different people pulling them in different directions that they didn't know who or what was right anymore. That's what made even the best of them inconsistent and uncertain. But I notice that nobody has ever tried to punish those busybodies. At least my intent was not to seize power for power's sake, or for petty advantages such as prestige and opportunities for corruption. It was to have order in this country at last.

Notwithstanding that, I know what I did was dishonest and therefore wrong, Your Honour. So let us get on with the sentence. I won't object to your destroying the robot, if that's what you think is right. I only hope that we'll be able to find a worthy human replacement for him soon. Someone who can maintain the peace, efficiency, and prosperity that we have achieved under my robot's order.

Yes, I am done and I apologize for talking so long. But still, I do not apologize for creating our very first android president.

4

By the Light of the Moon

Each night he lay with a goddess of silvery glow. It was not like being with any other woman, not that Roel Datu had actually lain with too many other women in the biblical sense in his lifetime. Mathematics majors who were aspiring astrophysicists rarely spent much time in female company. Certainly they were not known for being ladies' men. As concerned as he was over the proposal he was preparing for his application for the doctoral astrophysics program of a prominent U.S. institution, Roel was fully aware how fortunate he was and did not struggle much against the temptation to lie with her every night.

It was not prudery that made him resort to this term— well, a little perhaps, but mainly it was his geeky tendency towards extreme precision of language. He didn't do so much as take off his pyjamas. He just lay there. But he never actually slept during these encounters; how could he? When she merged her non-corporeal form with his slight, unimpressive human one he felt a chill and yet felt heat build up inside him as he was immersed in her cool light. It built up until there was a supernova within him. He lay gasping, spent for some moments once it exploded, then he sat up slowly, invigorated by the steady glow within him.

He gently ran his hand over the pulsing, glowing mass of light on his bed. Then he got up and went to take a shower, hoping the next-door neighbour he barely knew wasn't back home from the call centre where she worked. If she was, she'd hear him and probably wonder why he was showering in the middle of the night. Once dressed, he went to his computer, switched it on, and got to work revising his paper. He sat staring at the screen now as it glowed on. He read his introduction:

> *Based on data from various studies and my own calculations, it is my theory that the Earth was once a gas giant with multiple moons like Jupiter and Saturn. These multiple moons, all but one, were diverted into the asteroid belt by Mars as the Earth's orbit weakened in the process of settling into the stable body that it is today.*

'As stable a body as yours?' murmured a silky voice. The glowing female form on the bed shifted and stretched.

He glanced over at her and smiled. He didn't have his glasses on as his myopia didn't impair his ability to read his computer screen, but he knew that even if he donned them she would still look to him like a vaguely female-shaped, moonlight-soft blur.

'More stable than yours, certainly,' he said. He felt a tingle of excitement as he remembered how she had warmed him, stirred his molecules, and blended into him and he hurriedly turned his eyes back to the screen. Too late. His concentration was shot.

He swivelled his chair towards the nightstand, picked up his glasses and wiped the lenses. They always steamed up when she came close to him.

He remembered the night he had first met her. It was the night of the supermoon and he had gone out to the riverside park near his condo so he could look at it. His eyes on the enormous white moon, he had walked all the way to the edge of the river. He felt a pair of eyes on him and became aware that a policeman nearby had his eyes on him.

'I'm not planning to throw myself in the river,' he reassured the officer. He gestured towards the moon. 'Just looking at the supermoon.'

He had hardly spoken to anyone all weekend, having holed himself up working on his application proposal. He started to babble, sharing all the facts he knew about the supermoon—and they were considerable. He'd read up on it quite a bit. The officer smiled amiably and went on his way. Alone once more, Roel gazed up at the moon for some time, then studied its reflection in the water. He idly kicked a stone into the water.

To his amazement, the reflection of moonlight rose and drew itself up, taking the form of a blindingly beautiful naked woman. She spoke to him in a silvery, commanding voice, saying, 'While being stoned causes me no pain, I would prefer to be treated with dignity.'

'I apologize,' Roel said, his eyes wide with astonishment. He took his glasses off and wiped them. Settling them back on his nose, he saw the ethereal creature was still there. 'I meant no disrespect. I was unaware there was anyone there,' he added humbly.

She eyed him warily. 'I am always on my guard when bathing on your planet and so I often camouflage myself by staying in the reflection of moonlight.'

'I can see why,' Roel said, taking in her luminescent pallor.

He was not a believer in supernatural beings and from her statement he derived that she had come from another planet. This thrilled but did not surprise him. He had been fascinated with outer space all his life and fervently believed that there were extra-terrestrial beings that were capable of traveling to the Earth. No, he was not surprised to find one at last, nor frightened. The thudding of his heart within his chest was a sign, rather, of delight at the opportunity and determination not to waste it.

'Tell me about yourself. You are very beautiful,' he added quickly.

She smiled. Clearly even aliens were not immune to flattery. 'In this form, I am. But if I wish, I may take this form.' And suddenly her features grew monstrous. Her eyes grew large and bugged out and glowing white fangs protruded from her mouth above a lolling white tongue. Roel started, but soon recovered.

'You are a shapeshifter, I see. May I see more proof of your amazing power?'

She laughed and turned herself back into a beautiful woman with the addition of pale wings sprouting from her back. She fluttered around him and swirled around faster and faster, until she was a diaphanous whirlwind around him. Then suddenly she dropped back into the water as a gleaming white swan.

'That is in case anyone is watching. So we may continue our conversation without anyone remarking on it. Or me.'

'Swans are uncommon here,' he pointed out. 'You might still attract too much attention that way.' He thought of suggesting she take the form of a duck, but he could not see this graceful being as a duck or a goose.

She crawled up to the bank as a thin, pale cat. 'Better?' she purred.

He nodded hastily. 'What are you?' Roel asked in awe, then quickly corrected himself. 'Who are you, I mean. I'm Roel Datu, mathematician and aspiring astrophysicist.'

'I go by many names,' she replied. 'As many as my forms. But I favour the name of Haliya, sister and protectress of the moon God.' And she reared up as a woman again this time with long, menacing fingernails and a flaming sword in one hand.

'I see,' he said, and satisfied, she melted back into the form of a cat. Though, truth be told, he didn't really see at all. Growing up as a fact-oriented child, he had never taken much interest in folklore. He made a mental note to read up on the mythical figure of Haliya.

Gazing back up at the moon, he started talking about some studies he had read about and some strange anomalies about the moon that he was seeking to form a theory to explain. She eagerly supported him, telling him about the earliest years of the Earth. He hung on her every word, fascinated. Then suddenly she stopped. 'I am inconsiderate to elaborate on these matters for so long at this time of the night.'

'Not at all, tell me more! This is extremely helpful to me, Haliya.'

'I am pleased to be of help to you. But continuing now would not help you with *them*.' She turned her head slightly, and her grey cat's eyes glowered at some shadowy figures lurking nearby.

'What?' He followed her gaze. 'Oh. Well, that policeman must still be around here somewhere.'

'But where we can't say. And he may return too late.'

He saw the cloudy cat face distort, grow fierce, and begin to expand.

'That won't be necessary.' As the men moved toward him, he dug his wallet out of his right back pocket, flung it behind him and hurried off. He felt a quivering presence by his cheek—that cat had leaped onto his shoulder and stayed with him until he slowed to a walk outside his building.

'Why did you do that? I could have scared them away for you?'

'I didn't have too much money in my wallet, and no identification either. I figured it was a simple way to avoid any trouble. And keep them from noticing you.'

'What does that matter?'

He had reached his second-floor apartment by now, and unlocked it with the key attached to the leather card case that held his ATM and his driver's license. 'I think you may be too bold for your own good. Am I the first person you've appeared to over thousands of years?'

'No.'

'And how have the others reacted upon seeing you?'

'In recent years, not too well,' she admitted. 'Most people scream. Others whip out their phones and try to take photos and videos. You're different.'

'I've always been different.' He sat on the edge of his bed to take off his shoes. It was closer to the door than his only other seating, his desk chair.

'I mean it in a good way.'

She was back in her human form now, and he saw her smiling at him. He smiled back, reached out a hand, then laughed.

'Why?'

'If I had gone out and met a human girl that I enjoyed talking to as much as I did with you, I'd probably say good night to her with a hug. A warm handshake, at the very least. And I can't even touch you. I mean, you were sort of on me earlier and I barely felt a thing. I suppose my hand would go right through you.'

'Not necessarily. I can control the density of my molecules. I can make myself dense enough to touch.' She drifted towards him. His skin prickled as she came closer. She held out a silvery-white hand to him and he took it. It was like touching a smooth, rushing rivulet of water. Then she grew paler, more transparent and added, 'I can also spread my particles, immerse you in them and let them enter you. Would you like that?'

'Intriguing,' he said hoarsely. 'How?'

She turned nearly invisible and he reached out to her in a panic, fearing she was disappearing completely. Then suddenly, he felt himself enveloped by a cool, soothing glow. He gasped and collapsed on his bed.

Roel found himself alone in the morning, but after a whole day convincing himself it was just a dream conjured up by his lonely, love-starved mind, he received another visit from her the following night. He was delighted.

'I never got to thank you,' he said.

'Thank me for what?'

'For—you know.' He flushed and said instead, 'You may have saved my life. And you also helped me to think of this.' He gestured towards the draft of his theory on the screen of his laptop. He rambled on excitedly until she convinced him to lie down and get some rest. She blanketed him and after a while—a long thrilling while—he actually did sleep. It wasn't for long, so he was surprised at how energized he felt as she waved goodbye to him at his window at sunrise.

As she continued to visit him every night, he grew as entranced and obsessed with her as with the astronomical facts he had learned from her. In between his extensive scientific research, he also googled a bit and posted some questions on his social media about the early Filipino goddess Haliya. What he had learned was fascinating. A beautiful mythical figure who hid her blindingly lovely face behind a frightening mask, the better to accomplish her role of protecting the moon, her brother. Occasionally seen bathing on Earth, she was a fierce fighter who had defeated the *bakunawa,* the sea serpent that had attempted to devour her fearful brother, the last of the seven moons.

'All stories, except for the parts about bathing and the seven moons,' she laughingly replied, when he mentioned them to her the next time she returned. 'I mingled more with the people of the Earth in centuries past. I shared some of my knowledge with them as I did with you, and that was the convoluted result. I certainly didn't mind being called a goddess, though. It was one of the things I loved most about living in your country. Along with all your beautiful coves to bathe in and your great variety of bodies of water to enjoy.'

'You like to swim a lot, huh?'

'It is not just a pleasure but a necessity for me. All living beings need water, as you know. And the beings of my kind are no exception. But since we do not eat and drink as you do, we must immerse ourselves in it and absorb water into our being.'

'Just like when you immerse yourself in me?' he asked slyly.

'Not at all!' she protested. 'That is a different matter entirely. When we are immersed in each other we create new energy, which we share.'

'I did kind of feel that. How does that happen?'

Her shoulder shifted upwards, as if in a shrug. 'It is a mystery. It may be the miracle of what you Earthlings call love.'

He laughed. He didn't know if this was love, but he did feel incredibly lucky to be visited by her every night since that night by the river. After spending all his free time in the days that followed in research, he was convinced what she had told her about the existence of other moons in the past was plausible. He was thrilled. If he could prove it, he could make quite a name for himself.

He had been at loose ends ever since he had finished his master's degree. When he completed his bachelor's he took a job as an IT consultant because it paid well and was near the university where he had already applied for the master's program. In the succeeding years, his days had been full as he was working all day and studying all night. With those years of study done, now his days were a drab routine of meaningless number-crunching all day. It was a far cry from what the life he had dreamed of as a child. So he had chosen to reach for the stars. Now, thanks to Haliya, he could construct an impressive research proposal and enter a course that could lead to greater things.

'You're the only one I can talk to about my real interests,' he told her gratefully as she appeared one evening.

'You're about the only one I can talk to, too,' she smiled back as she reposed on his bed in her graceful female form.

'Aren't there any others of your kind?' he asked suddenly.

'We are not exactly sociable. We are perhaps what you call territorial? We each occupy our own particular space on this planet.'

'Where is your home planet?'

'This is home now. But once it was there.' And she pointed one translucent figure towards the evening star.

'Venus?'

'Once upon a time, when it had water. As it dried up, we escaped its weak magnetic field and made our way to the next planet. At least those of us who were strong enough to survive the long trip without water. Water is life to us.'

'To us, too.'

'Indeed. And that is why you are very fortunate to still have your seas and rivers.'

'I'd love to see you bathe in a waterfall,' he said, running his hand gently over her form. If he applied pressure his hand would go right through, so it was like running his hand on the surface of water, except her surface resisted him with a faint tingling warmth rather than clinging to his palm when he passed it along her outline. It really was like touching strong flowing water. 'There are some lovely falls I've read about not too far from here,' he told her. 'Where I grew up in the province, there was a waterfall near our home. I enjoyed sitting on the rocks below and feeling the water pour down on me on hot days. My older brother liked diving into the pool from the top of the falls. I was always afraid to. He teased me for that.' He shook his head at the memory.

'You have family,' she said in a wistful tone.

'Sure. Most people do. But I'm not close to mine. Well, I was to my mother, but she died a few years back. My father always liked my brother better. They're both athletic and they run a chain of sports shops in our provincial capital. They have no interest in me or what I do at all. My brother doesn't even really thank me for the science toys and math games I send his kids, though his wife always sends me photos showing them enjoying them.'

'When I observe the difficulties humans have in their relationships, sometimes it makes me glad that my kind have little to do with each other,' she mused. 'But it can get lonely. At least for me. I would like to have a child, but ultimately that wouldn't make a difference.'

'You reproduce then?'

'Yes. Two or more of us can merge into each other and create a new life form that is a blend of each parent's attributes. But as we are immortal as long as well-supplied with water, and as I said, not very sociable, we feel very little urgency for reproduction. In any case, our offspring, once produced, will merely float away like clouds.'

'How sad.' He felt no particular hurry to have children but once he did he wouldn't want his relationship with them to be like what he had with his father and brother.

Though admittedly having no strong attachments had its advantages. Once he got home from work, he had few interruptions unless you counted the messages that appeared on his social media. He found it easy to ignore these, only stopping now and then to check the news, both international and more personal, such as a post shared by his brother about the new advanced science and math program they were starting at their old high school. Then he worked relentlessly on his proposal. He included all the supporting data he could find. But of course he was careful not to mention Haliya. He just had to hope he could sound convincing without citing her as an eyewitness.

The proposal sent to several prestigious institutions, Haliya proposed that he reward himself by going on a trip with her to a beach or at least the nearby falls. He said, 'There's nothing to celebrate yet. They haven't accepted me yet.'

'You still deserve it for working so hard. Come, let's go somewhere new.'

'What for? It's too much trouble. I have everything I need right here.' And he switched on his computer. 'Watch a movie with me.'

'Pictures are not terribly interesting to me seeing how much time I spend traveling, exploring, and observing your country by day,' she said with a touch of disdain.

'I thought you were nocturnal,' he said.

'Not at all. I only appear to you at night because I am only visible in the dark, being made up of just water and light. I do not need that much rest. I spend most of my time awake and active.'

'So you could hover around me all day with no one seeing you?'

'Yes, but I don't care to do it in that box you call your office.'

'I can understand that. I don't enjoy it too much there either. But one has to earn a living. And my mother got diagnosed with cancer shortly before I got my undergrad degree. So I decided to take a high-paying job right away to help out.'

'But I understand she is gone. And you do not seem happy there. So why do you stay?'

'Well, of course, money, benefits. And there's this condo, which is tiny and nothing special but it's near work. It's what I spend most of my salary on. I have to pay it off, you know . . .' He trailed off and laughed ironically. 'I guess you wouldn't know. You're lucky to be able to live so simply. So free.'

'I do feel lucky to be free,' she reflected. 'I don't care to remain in this box you live in for more than a few hours at a time. I don't see how you can bear it. Why don't you go away with me?'

'I have what I need here. I can relax and be comfortable.'

'Is that really all you want?' She shook her head in bemusement. 'Once, when I was resting in a pool outside a restaurant, I heard some women laughing and saying that men were from Mars and women were from Venus. I didn't know what they meant then.'

He couldn't help laughing. In this case, the woman really was from Venus.

'I think I understand now,' she continued.

'You know that I'm not from Mars, right?'

'Yes. But you still want different things from me.' She gazed at him steadily. 'If you don't care to go with me, I think I will take a little trip myself.'

'Sorry, I just really need a break right now,' he apologized. 'But if all goes well, my life will change pretty soon. Though maybe not that much. The schools I applied to are in cities as congested and polluted as Manila, I understand. Cleaner though, I think, and closer to the sea. You'd like that, wouldn't you?'

'Are you inviting me to go with you?'

'Well, if I make it, I hope you would. I don't expect to have a lot of spare time, of course. There's going to be a lot of hard work.'

'Why do you want to do that, then?' she asked.

'I guess I just want to realize my potential. Just do more, be more than I am now. Because I can.' He shrugged. 'I don't really know where I'll be going with that degree. I guess I really just want to prove myself, especially to my dad and brother who never thought much of me. It's a guy thing. And I really do like to stay cooped up with my computer. I guess you don't understand that.'

She nodded curtly. 'I expect I'll just go on a trip on my own,' she said, and swept out into the night.

He watched his moonlit creature flit off, with a touch of envy. She was so free, so sure of what she wanted. Of course she'd had millennia to find her identity and wasn't subject to human struggles as he was. He wasn't sure what he wanted to do with his life, only that he wanted to escape from his current state. If only doing that was as easy for him as floating out a window was for her.

Haliya had forgotten how much she enjoyed traveling freely throughout the islands. For weeks, she had remained in the city to be near Roel. There were many interesting sights and sufficient clean sources of water there but leaving it for the wide open spaces of the farmlands and the coastline was refreshing. She rode on river rapids and rolling ocean waves. It was delightful. But eventually, traveling on her own grew lonely. Especially since every time she was sighted by humans they reacted with fright and called her some horrible name, then ran off before she could inform them what she truly was. Rising from a rice paddy at twilight, she had startled two children collecting fireflies, who ran away screaming they had seen the man-eating creature of horror, the aswang. Once she was bathing in a fountain in a plaza when it suddenly turned off, exposing her to a few passers-by who shuddered and gasped and screamed that they had seen a white lady—and she knew they were not just remarking on her pallor. Why was it that as people let go of their belief in the supernatural they still continued to hang on to the negative myths yet quickly discarded the positive? Nobody saw her as a tree spirit or sky maiden now as they did hundreds of years ago. Nobody even thought of her as an angel, maybe because they saw her at night, and despite all the lighting in the modern world, the innate fear of the night persisted. And so everyone saw her as a ghost or worse. Nobody else she had met had displayed the matter-of-fact courage of Roel and made the effort to learn who and what she was.

And so, she eventually returned to the one person she had entrusted with the true story of her origins. The only one who had ever listened to her and really tried to get to know her.

The sun had just set when she slipped into his room, but already he was lying in bed, fully dressed in his work clothes. She kept herself concealed at first in the glow of the streetlight against the window. She wanted to observe him, see how he had been doing without her, before she showed herself to him.

The sight of him lying in bed at this time puzzled her. Of course, she didn't normally visit him as early as this. Perhaps it was his habit to rest as soon as he came home from work. There was so much she didn't know about humans. And about him.

Suddenly, she heard a thud as he pounded his fist on the nightstand. Once, then many, many times. She swiftly went to his side.

'Shh,' she said gently. 'Why are you doing this?'

'They not only all rejected me immediately, they laughed at me! They called it an absurd premise based on a clumsy assembled collection of evidence. Nobody can believe my theory about the changes in the Earth and our moons!' He rolled over and groaned in frustration.

She did not possess human anatomy, being constructed purely of energy, water, and light. But she felt a quiver within her like the quickening of his heart when she consumed him. His pain was her pain, and she only thought of how to relieve it.

'There's only one thing to do then,' she said softly. 'Tell me where to find them and I will go to them and tell them what I told you. They'd believe it coming directly from me, won't they?'

'You'd do that for me?' He sat up quickly.

'Of course.'

'Thank you, Haliya. That means a lot to me. But, no, no . . .' He shook his head vigorously. 'No, you can't!' He reached for her hands and attempted to clasp them. His hands went right through and formed tight fists instead. 'It will be dangerous for you.'

'Those of my kind occupying the territory can be made to understand.'

'I mean, if the people of the institute do believe you were what you say you were, they may not let you go. They'll want to study you, keep you as proof of existence of extra-terrestrial life.'

'No walls can keep me in!' she declared.

'But they will hound you and search for you. They will not leave you in peace. And who knows if they might find a way to capture you, even hurt you? I couldn't let that happen.'

Again a quiver within her, this time a warm stirring. 'Why not?' she asked.

'Why do you think, Haliya? I care about you. You—you mean a lot to me. Nothing seemed right when you were gone.'

'Is this what you Earthlings call love?' she said teasingly.

'I think so.' There was a hint of surprise in his voice, as if he had just realized it at that moment. 'I haven't really experienced it before with a girl. I've liked some but it never lasted long. It wasn't like this. What we have, how we feel, it all seems to fit with how love is always shown to be. You mean more to me than my old dream.'

'Your old dream? So you have a new one already?'

'Yes.' He lovingly traced the outline of her face with his hand. 'It's to be with you.'

Tenderly, she enveloped him with her cooling energy. 'Do you really mean that? After you worked so hard—'

'Yes.' He sighed deeply. 'None of that matters to me anymore, as long as you are with me,' he murmured. 'Please don't leave me again.'

She grew still. 'I can't promise that entirely. I need to be free to roam.'

'I understand. Because, you know what? So do I.' He sat up. 'This is not how I grew up and this is not what I dreamed of being when I was growing up. I grew up in a town with plenty of open space and clean bodies of water. And dreamed of doing something great for the world. Maybe I can't do it as an astrophysicist yet. But I can do something meaningful right now. I'm a fool and a coward to stay in a job that doesn't make me happy, that's only about making money for a company I don't value highly. I'm going to leave it, and go somewhere where you and I can live happily together.'

'Where?' she asked.

'I'll start by going to my old school. I'll apply to teach in their new advanced mathematics program. I'll feel more of a sense of purpose teaching, anyway, than in my job now. We can visit the waterfall I played in as a child every day. We'll have some semblance of the life of a happy couple.'

She knew what he meant. He would keep her a secret; he had to. She was satisfied with that. 'It sounds wonderful,' she said. 'Only . . . we won't have children.'

'It doesn't really matter to me. Does it to you?'

Slowly she withdrew from him and lay nestled beside him. She was still, considering.

'In any case, do you know for certain it is impossible for us to have one?'

'It has never happened before,' she told him.

'Have we ever happened before?' he asked, gazing right at her.

'No,' she conceded.

It had never happened before, a being from the planet they called Venus being with an Earthling in this way. Not as far as she knew. But she meant too that she had never felt this warm sensual prickling of her particles in another's presence, the desire to at once consume and to lose herself in him. She settled herself over him, blanketing him, a cloud of cooling energy, soothing him, stirring, until he cried out and she echoed him. She lingered around him, quivering gently sighing in the wake of an explosion that had shaken her whole being.

As she rested gently beside him, she saw it: A pale misty glowing mass, a smaller but denser version of herself drifting towards the window.

She beckoned to it. To her surprise, it drifted towards her. And as she crooned to it of the rhythmic rush of waterfalls and the gentle rains, it settled between her and her sleeping Earthling.

5

The Sincerest Form of Flattery

When I was eight, my parents decided they wanted to have another child. My mother was forty-four, but what did it matter? There were numerous options open to her. Since my parents were determined that the child should be one hundred percent 'theirs'—no donor eggs—they opted for cloning.

I didn't know it then, but human cloning was a highly illegal underground industry. Perhaps if I had not been so busy brooding about what it would be like to lose my honoured place as the baby of the family, the only actual child when I was growing up, really, as my half-brother was twelve years older than me—perhaps, innocent as I was then, I would have sensed it in a way from my parents' tension, their constant warnings, their silencing glares when company arrived in the middle of a discussion about the cloning—all that, now that I look back on it, were signs that they were engaged in something not quite right.

They did pick up on my animosity towards the potential new sibling, so they decided to have me present during their meeting with the 'doctor' who was to perform the procedure. He wasn't really a doctor, the woman who had referred us to him had explained. He was a brilliant but rebellious medical student who had never gotten his degree but learned his trade by working in labs throughout the world, most of them illegal cloning facilities. I had expected him to look like a mad scientist from a cartoon, but he was just an ordinary-looking young man. I later realized that the gleam in his eye was not unlike the mad scientist's. But at that time, seeing that he didn't look anything special, I immediately lost interest in him and all that he had to say.

I sat hunched in a chair that was too big for me while the doctor explained the procedure to me, and why my mother couldn't have a baby in the same way she'd had me. He said he was using simple terms, but most of it was still over my head. Not that I made much effort to understand. When he was done, my parents smiled at me. 'There, you see, Lorrayne, you'll always be special to us. You are our one hundred percent natural girl,' my father said.

I thought that the baby was going to be special too. It would be the one they chose. It would turn out exactly like they planned. They would know exactly what it wanted and they would be sure to give those things to it. Or him. Or her?

'Will it be a boy or a girl?' I asked.

'A girl,' my mother answered before anyone else could speak. 'We are going to clone your grandmother, my mother.'

I gasped. 'But Grandma is still alive—sort of.' Horrifying as it sounded, that was the most accurate way I could put it, in my eight-year-old way. My grandmother had been on life support for the past four years, following a stroke which had left her brain dead. What to do about her condition had long been a source of debate among my mother and her brother and sister. My mother could not bear to take her off life support and being the eldest, her word was law, though the other two might rebel by delaying their contributions to the hospital expenses.

My father was saying to the doctor, 'It's what she wants, though I find it strange myself. I mean, a woman being mother to her own mother.'

'It's not like that. We've been through this before,' my mother said. 'It's the only way that I'll ever feel right letting my mother go.'

'When she was around, you couldn't stand her—all her criticism, her demands. You left the country to get away from her. You complained those few years when you came back and had to stay with her because she couldn't look after her house by herself and she refused to move. She never liked me, either, no matter what I did for her. And now you want her back as your child?' My father raised his voice, and I remembered their long arguments which had sounded much the same.

'I've felt guilty about my feelings towards her ever since she had her stroke, you know that. But it's more than that. I have been thinking about how she came to be that way. You know I've been going over her old documents recently. And I found some letters and diaries that told about her childhood. She never did speak much about her family, and it seems that her parents had a stormy relationship, always quarrelling violently, and her father was an abusive alcoholic. Maybe she could have gotten over that completely once she was happily married if it hadn't been for my father's tragic death. All that could make anyone unhappy and warp them emotionally. But now I can give her the happy childhood that she never had, and we can discover what a wonderful woman she would have been with the proper guidance and care. Wouldn't that be wonderful, to have a grandchild to imitate the best in her, to pass on her legacy? It's the ultimate act of love.'

'Imitation is the sincerest form of flattery, my teacher says,' I put in. She had said that when I'd quarrelled with a classmate of mine who was always buying exactly the same new accessory I had just shown off in school. Though when I said it the time she caught me copying from my seatmate's paper, she took away my paper and made me sit in a corner till the test was over. So maybe it wasn't always true.

From the looks of my father, maybe it wasn't true for this situation. He ignored me, responding only to my mother's words. 'Remember, I only agreed to that on the condition that we change some of her traits so she won't be exactly like your mother. My line should be represented too, you know.' He turned to the doctor. 'We're hoping you can help us decide.'

I didn't want a brother or sister, so I was secretly pleased that they couldn't agree. Maybe they would call the whole thing off.

For a while, it seemed they would. They couldn't agree that afternoon, though every sentence that oozed out of their mouths in phonily honeyed tones seemed to be prefaced with 'I thought we agreed that . . .' They thought they agreed the baby would look like my mom (I looked more like Dad) and that she would be tall—though not too tall as that could be a disadvantage for a girl in some ways (except that the other parent thought they agreed that it wasn't). The last argument was repeated when it came to intelligence; just replace the words tall with 'smart' and 'good at math'.

I fell asleep in the midst of that discussion, and they had to shake me awake and whisk me home, where they continued the argument the moment they put me in bed. When I woke up, I found my prayers hadn't been answered. They had made their decisions and written them down to be sent to the doctor before they changed their minds again. I later found out that they had tossed a coin on some of the questions. I thought that was a rather childish way of settling things, and not nearly as well-planned as they said it would be, but they said that it was better than leaving things entirely to chance. They were so exhilarated as they faxed the copy that they didn't notice me storm off. Did they really think they could hide from me the fact that they thought I, their random daughter, wasn't good enough?

Over the next nine months, instead of speculating, as I've observed other prospective parents do about their offspring (Will it be a boy or a girl? Who will it look like?), my parents read and reread the list of child-to-come's traits—and worried about them. Would her high verbal ability conflict with her equally high musical and mathematical skills? Would she be so smart as to be intimidating to boys, so creative as to get bored with a steady job? Would all the different talents they chose for her cancel each other out, so she'd be some kind of jack-of-all-trades, master of none? It made me wonder why they even wanted another kid, if she would only be a worry to them. Mom said all children were a worry, but they at least knew they didn't have to worry about adjusting to this one, because they would know in advance what she'd be like, and be prepared. This made me wonder just how much they had worried about me, but I didn't bother to ask.

They were so excited about the upcoming birth that they didn't notice that I was withdrawing from them, spending more time shut up in my room or at the homes of neighbourhood friends. They didn't notice my reluctance to talk about the sister to come—or perhaps they were simply relieved at my silence, since they had some apprehensions about their contracting an illegal service being known. Of course, a lot of people did it, and probably many others would have too if they'd only been rich enough. But the government retained its conservative stance. I really only surmised that they were anxious about this, never confirmed, since the day they decided to have their custom-made child, I stopped talking to my parents about my feelings. They didn't want to listen anyway.

And then my sister, named Rebecca after Grandma, arrived. And from that day my parents' attention revolved around her. They raved about her looks—she had my grandmother's fair skin and delicate frame and my mother's pretty almond-shaped eyes, while I was dark-skinned and sturdy like my father. Later they also delighted over her love for cooking (again from Grandma), her interest in science (mostly from my dad), her tuneful voice (from Mom) and her athletic skill (this from my father entirely). These were traits I shared too, but did anyone notice? No. Nobody did.

Even my half-brother, when he came home from his college abroad to visit, focused all his attention on Rebecca.

I reminded him of his promises in all his emails to play with me and take me on outings. He laughed and told me that if I would stop being so whiny he would spend more time with me. I was furious. Why blame me? Didn't I have a right to feel bad at the lack of attention? But then it seemed I was always in the wrong ever since Rebecca arrived, even when she was too little to do anything. And things only became worse as she grew older and became conscious of her charm. And so, as we grew older, my resentment grew too.

But I also found, in my adolescent years, that the lack of parental attention was somewhat to my advantage. At fourteen and fifteen, I had the freedom few of my classmates had to stay out, go places, sleep over at a friend's, and date.

Well, I wasn't entirely free. My parents did object those times when they caught me sneaking in late smelling of cigarette smoke, kissing a boy on our doorstep, or coming in at five a.m. on a school day to change my clothes before going to school (at least I never skipped school or flunked. I had about as high an IQ as that they'd given little Rebecca, so school was a breeze for me, even when I didn't study).

My parents would question me those times, and scold me. But their words failed to touch me. I knew it wasn't me they were concerned about. After all, what did they say? 'Have some respect for your parents!' 'What will the neighbours think?' or worse 'Think of the example you're setting for your little sister!'

Inwardly I would answer: 'Respect for my parents? Why, when you don't really act as parents to me?' and 'Yeah, what will the neighbours think of you as parents—that's all you really care about!' And, 'Why should you worry about the example I'm setting for Rebecca? She was created perfect, remember?'

But as I said, I had long stopped talking to them, stopped expecting them to listen. So I would simply sail past with a smirk and go my own way.

Anyway, I shaped up of my own volition in my last couple of years of school, but then most of my friends did too. We were determined we wouldn't be stuck in our parents' homes for life. We were going to go to college somewhere far off and board together, then later get jobs that would allow us to live on our own.

I researched on the Internet in the early mornings, the only time when that bratty Rebecca wasn't hogging our computer to 'do her homework.' Most of the time, she was just playing—but my parents believed she needed to do puzzles and create pictures to develop her intelligence and creativity, so she still got away with it! I knew it was useless to argue anyway, so I simply waited for her to go to bed. I read all I could about colleges and careers that interested me and dreamed of becoming a journalist, hopefully writing for travel publications so I would get to go all over the world. And I actually became a conscientious student.

My parents didn't notice what I was doing, it seemed. They never asked about my plans. I suppose they took it for granted I would enrol in the university where my mother taught music, to take advantage of the tuition discount. They were more interested in their precocious younger daughter, already at just ten years old proclaiming to the world that she was going to be a doctor, the doctor my grandmother hadn't become. Grandma had actually gone to a medical school for a year, but she was married to my grandfather already by then, and when she got pregnant she found it impossible to continue. I had overheard my parents talking about how, when she was alive (I mean really alive, of course, but she wasn't even on life support anymore, since with little ceremony they had pulled the plug when Rebecca was two), she would sneer at my father for having failed one science course after the other while she had gone to medical school early and might have finished if my mother hadn't arrived in her second year. She knew these things because she taught in the college of science where Dad had gone, and she had made it her business to investigate his background when he got engaged to Mom.

That was one story that made me glad I hadn't really known Grandma, and that I wasn't supposed to be like her. To be sure, Rebecca was supposed to be an improvement on Grandma, growing up with all the advantages. But it seemed to me she had just as many of those annoying traits of Grandma's I'd heard about. Certainly, Becca was nosy— listening in on my phone conversations, entering my room and getting my things when I wasn't home. Locking up was no use because she could go to my parents' room to get their copy of my room key. Mom didn't mind if Rebecca tried on her clothes or played with her make-up and thought I shouldn't mind either. When I'd see Rebecca wearing some of my bead jewellery and snatch it away, Mom would reprove me, saying, 'You should be glad you have a little sister who admires you so much she wants to dress like you, Lorrayne.' Well, what did I expect? I just did my best to hide my things from Little Miss Perfect, but she still managed to find them wherever they were, and she just laughed in my face when I caught her snooping and rescued my things.

I also noticed that Rebecca would make fun of the girls who were supposed to be her friends. She and my mom would laugh together over the nasty stories she would tell about them, and go on about how superior Rebecca was to them in every way. Rebecca would cause trouble among her group of friends, making up stories about what one girl had said about another—the kind of thing, I knew, that my grandmother had done with all her children and their spouses once they were married.

But my parents were little concerned over this. All they could see was what was right about her, just as all they could see in me was what was wrong about me.

Of course, it's easy to find something if you already know it's supposed to be there.

So even if she was more than eight years younger, I hated her. I hadn't even been very comfortable with my grandmother. All I remembered of her was that she was cranky and always called me by the names of one of her daughters instead of my own. I was somewhat interested in learning what she was like when she was younger, but if young Rebecca really did have her personality, it wasn't any more charming than that of the senior Rebecca I had so briefly known. Though of course, toddlers are typically loud and demanding. Maybe she wouldn't have been so bad if my parents hadn't been so quick to indulge her. And they only reproached me when I complained. She, their made-to-order daughter, could do no wrong.

I tried to be her opposite, surprise them as only a random, natural child could. I had none of my mother's skill in music, unlike Rebecca, who was a natural. So I hoped to find in me some of my father's way with words as a professional social media influencer. I had grown mistrustful of his florid prose and charm when he exercised it to influence *me* out of my resentment ('Rebecca wears your clothes because she worships you! You can always get another shirt like that, but you can't replace your admiring little sister,' he once cajoled). So I wrote stark prose that presented facts truthfully, which didn't impress my parents but was seen by my teachers as a sign I had the makings of the journalist. I came to revel in the idea of distinguishing myself in a field which no one else in my family was in.

As I grew into my teens, I wanted so much to be rid of Rebecca and leave my parents who I'd felt had betrayed me. While it turned out that I ended up in journalism school in a neighbouring city, I was still determined to live on my own, and so I convinced my parents to let me rent a room with my friend Thessa by telling them I would study better if I wasn't tired out by a long commute. My parents agreed and didn't seem to mind paying for my rent, probably because I'd become so annoying by then that they were glad to get rid of me.

And so I missed my little sister's remaining growing-up years. My parents would call me now and then, trying to convince me to attend some family gathering, but I always made my excuses. I spent my holidays at the homes of friends. I didn't fool myself that my parents wanted *me*; I knew that they just wanted to fulfil the picture they had in their minds of the perfect family. And they put all the responsibility for that on—who else—me. I, the one born random and imperfect, was the one to blame for my family's imperfections. Of course.

Though I didn't ask, my parents kept me up to date on Rebecca's news. They were ecstatic over her acceptance into an integrated college and med school course, and were furious that I wouldn't take out time from my job as the travel section editor of a lifestyle magazine to attend her high school graduation, where they insisted she should have been at the top of the class. I let them rant about how the girl that the school had chosen as valedictorian over her was not half as deserving, that they'd only showed favouritism towards her because a newspaper story had come out about the girl's involvement in some community project. I told them cheerfully that I would be boycotting Becca's graduation to show my dissent at the school's choice of valedictorian. My parents were not amused. But they gave up trying to convince me to go.

But now I was finally going to them. Now that the news about Rebecca is far from good. My mother called me while I was having dinner with my friend Darin at the hottest new place in town, the first place here to offer the new smart entertainment—holographic singers who choose music to suit your mood. When she called, an elegant woman in shimmery blue appeared and began to croon something which I guess was supposed to soothe me while I rummaged through my bag, tossing aside my custom-formulated make-up and perfume to find my phone, which was ringing frantically with the customized emergency ring tone.

I opened the phone and met the eyes of my mother, whose tear-stained face filled the screen. The background music made it harder to hear, even though I had a headset, but there was no doubting my mother's words: 'Something has happened to Rebecca.'

The eight-year-old in me that had wished my sister dead even before she was born let out a hint of a hysterical laugh. 'How is that possible? How could anything have gone wrong with your perfect baby?' And I ripped off my headset, folded up the phone and turned back to Darin, seated across the table from me.

How to explain Darin? I didn't really think of him as my boyfriend. I didn't do serious relationships, never had. I went out with men until I was bored with them, which didn't take long. I didn't expect them to fall in love with me. I was determined not to fall in love with anyone. I had no real explanation for this. I guess it was mainly that I felt it was enough to have achieved my independence and I was happy with the way my life was. A love relationship could mean a lot of sacrifices, and I wasn't about to give up the way of life I had struggled to achieve and maintain.

Darin Yuseco was a freelance photographer. When I first saw his shots last year, they blew me away, and naturally, they ended up on my pages whenever I could find room. They looked amazing in 3D on our covers or in panoramic spreads. I knew about his family—everyone did. They were into every kind of business there was, it seemed, including publishing. I'd actually had a job interview with Darin's dad some years back, before Darin and I had met. He was cordial enough, even when he questioned me about my stance on the libel case that the paper was involved in at that time. At that time, being a fresh graduate desperate for a job, I had been determined to evade that issue, but put on the spot I blurted out that I felt that the paper had made some mistakes but I was sure they had learned from them and as a member of the staff I would be very, very careful. He looked amused at my naïvely bold comment and reached out to shake my hand, saying they'd call me. They didn't, of course, and I didn't care because I soon got a job with one of their competitors.

Ironically, Darin preferred to work with us rather than for any of his family's businesses. He preferred to live in his photography. Everyone thought he was crazy, except me. I couldn't help but see his similarity to me and wonder if his family situation was like mine. But I couldn't discuss that with him without discussing my own family, and that was something I was reluctant to do.

Now he was staring at me. I picked up my wine glass and he said, 'Are you sure you haven't had enough?'

It was hard to read his expression. 'My family situation is really complicated. I don't expect you to understand. But I assure you I would have acted that way even if I hadn't had a drop to drink. Maybe it's wrong, but that's how it is.'

'I won't judge you,' he said, 'until you've had a chance to explain.'

'But I won't explain,' I said, 'unless I can be sure you'll understand.'

'I don't have such a good relationship with my parents either,' he said. 'I'm the eldest son—'

'I know that.'

'Can you imagine what it's like, being the eldest son in such a family? My parents expected so much from me. They wanted me to be creative, a risk-taker, a good businessman.

Well, so I am. But I just don't want to exert my skills on behalf of any of our family endeavours. Luckily they have my younger brother, who seems to be leaning toward that direction. He's fifteen years younger than me, still in college, but he's closer to what they expected me to be.'

I reached over and placed my hand on top of his. 'That sounds a lot like my family,' I said, and I leaned over and told him the whole story, while we were serenaded with the most romantic songs by holographic guitarists all around. They probably had assumed from our closeness and the confidential tone of our voices that romance was brewing between us. Sometimes smart technology can be really dumb.

When I finished there was silence. No songs were heard. Perhaps our feelings were too confused for the hologram generators to adapt to.

'What would you do, if you were in my place?' I asked him.

'You don't have to forgive them, or become close to them, you know. Just be there for them. They're still your family.'

'I suppose you're right,' I said. I stood up. 'Will you come with me?'

I expected the police, who were talking to my father while my mother paced and tore at her hair. I expected my parents' not even noticing Darin, in their agitation, but I hadn't expected this: Perfect Rebecca had been discovered to have been selling drugs from the hospital to addicts. And now the police were looking for her, but my parents had no idea where she'd gone.

My mother kept saying, 'It must be a false accusation. Something a jealous friend made up. Rebecca would never do such a thing!'

I didn't know whether to be angry with her or feel sorry for her. I looked at my father instead. He looked angry too, and he seemed uncertain as to whether to believe the accusations or not.

The detective, a woman not much older than me, turned to me. 'Could we talk to you?'

At that moment my cell phone buzzed.

'Do you suppose that's your sister?' The detective asked.

'I doubt it. I don't think she even knows my number. We don't talk to each other. Never did.'

'Go ahead and answer it and see.'

I shrugged and took my phone from my pocket. I went to sit in a black recliner that hadn't been there when I was growing up. The detective didn't follow me, but she kept her eyes on me. Upon unfolding my phone, I noted the number on the screen. 'It's my roommate,' I called over my shoulder. Thessa probably just wanted to know how my date was going—she was that kind of person, one of those always insisting something was going on between me and Darin even if there wasn't. I put on the headset and answered the call. I was shocked to see my sister's face on the screen, with Thessa peering over her shoulder.

'Hey Lorrayne! Surprise, it's me. Where are you?'

'At home.'

'How can that be? I'm at your place—oh wait. You mean . . . you're with Mom and Dad?'

'Yes.'

'No! Well, just don't tell them where I am yet, okay? I'm just going to crash here for tonight. I'll be gone in the morning, promise. Your roommate wouldn't let me, though, unless I asked you first, so could you talk to her? She's right here.'

'Wait a minute. I'm not in the habit of harbouring fugitives from the law.'

A pause. Then a whisper. 'So Mom and Dad know?'

'So do the police.'

'Well, lie to them. Tell them you don't know where I am.'

I felt like slapping that face on the screen. 'What if they give me a lie detector test?' I hissed. 'Why should I put myself through all that trouble for your sake?'

'All right, all right, I'll go somewhere else so that when they ask you can honestly say you don't know. But I'll meet you at Grandma's grave at midnight. I'll email you a list of things to bring me. Bye.' And her face disappeared before I could refuse her the only favour she'd ever asked me. Whatever made her think she had the right to ask anything from me when I had lost all my parents' love to her?

Looking at the detective, I knew she surmised from my side of the conversation that I had spoken to my sister. All I told my parents and the police was that it was indeed my sister, but that she had gotten scared once she learned that the police were there and signed off. Immediately the detective went off to check the area near my apartment. I was unconcerned. With all the speedy forms of land and water transportation in the city, those networks of railways and waterways, she could be far away by the time they got there. Not that I cared whether she got away or not.

At least, I didn't care for her sake. But when I looked at the crumpled faces of my parents, I knew I had to keep my word to her, if only so I could assure them that she was all right.

Darin drove me to the cemetery on a hill just out of town. It was quite far out, but that was the only place for a cemetery now that the Manila area was so congested. The two of us wandered aimlessly over the grounds, triggering motion sensors all over the place to turn on lights, which went off again as we moved out of range. I had not been to my grandmother's grave in years, and I was not sure I could find it. But then, like a hologram, a pale waif-like woman with hair blowing around her face appeared with a sudden flash of motion-triggered light. 'Here I am,' she called. 'Did you bring the stuff?'

'I did.' I took the gym bag Darin was holding and went to hand it to her.

'I know you,' Rebecca said to Darin. 'I've seen your picture in the society pages. Well, well, and now you're with my sister. How did you ever hook such a guy, Lorrayne?'

'I didn't,' I said. As I handed her the bag, which I had stuffed with some of her clothes, a few provisions, and some mementos, I looked her up and down. I noted that she was wearing my new black trench coat—I recognized it from the pattern of iron-on crystals I'd applied myself—but I said nothing. She took the bag, sat down on the headstone, and started going through the contents of the bag. I sat on a bench across her, and Darin stood behind me.

'Aren't you going to explain yourself?' I asked. 'Can't you at least tell us why you did it?'

'Why do I do anything? I can't help what I do. It must be my heredity. Bet your Grandma did something similar once. She was pretty materialistic and not always that honest, I've heard, that's why she made such a success of Grandpa's business after he died. Some of our great-aunts think she only married him for his money, really, since the uncle who was putting her through med school had just died. I'm inclined to believe that. How else do you explain why she'd spurned him for ten years then suddenly just ran off and married him?' She looked up at me and grinned. 'Notice she isn't exactly reaching up from six feet under to strangle me. Nor do I feel anyone turning over underneath. It must be true.'

I just stared at her, horror-struck. She continued to rummage through the bag. 'What's this?' she said, holding up some CDs.

'Picture and video discs. Family pictures. I thought that wherever you are, you might want to look at them once in a while. They're mostly of you.'

She tossed them into my lap. 'Keep them. I don't want anything to do with the family anymore. I'm going off to live my own life, the way you did.'

'Don't you care?' I cried. 'They always loved you so, their lives revolved around you. You can't just forget about them like that.'

'They love me? Sure, those parts of me that they planned on. But everything wrong about me they disown, when the way I turned out is entirely their responsibility!'

The eight-year-old urge to kill my little sister was returning.

Darin went to her. 'Listen, Rebecca, I know how you feel.'

'How can you possibly—'

'You see,' Darin went on, 'I'm a clone too, a modified one. Like you.'

My sister and I stared at him.

'I was cloned from my father, only they made me even more intelligent and creative and even more of a risk-taker. You see, they wanted me not only to maintain the family empire but to develop and expand it. Well, by the time I was in my teens they could see their plans had somehow backfired. They couldn't make me do what they wanted me to do. So they had my brother, this time a perfect clone of my father. He really is a clone. He has no mind of his own where my father is concerned and now they worry that he won't be able to think on his own, that once my father dies he just won't be able to manage our corporation. He just doesn't have the courage to make his own decisions. My father does, of course, but I guess since Dad always had the kind of ideas he would have thought of first, my brother never developed the same ability.'

'What's the point of all this?' Rebecca muttered.

'The point is, that for all their playing God, there is a part of us that still develops in directions they couldn't foresee. It isn't all about genetics. It's about environment, too, and experiences and some mysterious elements. Perhaps you could call it destiny. And they can't rid us of that essential part of us called free will. I don't know where that resides really, but I don't think it has much to do with genetics.'

We were all silent for a moment. Then I said, 'You know, it doesn't matter why you did it. We all make stupid mistakes. This is a really bad one, but what matters is that you do right from now on. If you turn yourself in,' I added softly, 'you'll get a lighter penalty. Not death, anyway. And we'd stand by you still and visit you. I know we can get Mom and Dad to understand.'

'I'd rather exert my free will in other directions, thank you. I'm going. Goodbye. I'll be fine. I've got a car. You don't need to know where I got it.'

My sister turned and walked away. I started after her, then stopped beneath a tree, watching her until she was out of sight.

Darin joined me under the tree. The lights behind us switched off, now that we were both out of range, so we had nothing but the stars and the gibbous moon for light. I could see just the faintest gleam of the discs in my hands.

'Why didn't you tell me?' I asked Darin.

'You're a journalist, and I'm always wary around journalists. I don't like my family, but I still don't want to reveal anything that would hurt them.'

'Was it really so bad, being cloned?'

'I guess it was mostly my parents. There wasn't so much difference between the way they treated me and my brother and the way they treated my three older sisters. They expected a lot from the girls too because of all the lessons they were enrolling them in and the toys and clothes they were buying them. They were disappointed when the girls turned out to hate piano or to be afraid of horses or to be too inflexible for ballet or when they didn't do well in school or had the wrong sort of friends. But they learned to accept them as they are, and love them unconditionally. In my case, they see me as a failed experiment of a sort. They never loved me unconditionally—how could they, when they'd created me to fulfil their conditions for a perfect son? I was planned to be an extension of themselves, only better.'

'Well, what else is a child meant to be anyway?'

'A person in his own right, meant to open parents' minds to new things, to challenge them to love someone who is different? Don't they say you can't choose your own family— but you're meant to love them anyway? So that must be why.'

I gazed at the distant lights of the city. 'I certainly didn't choose my sister. I don't know if I love her, but I certainly worry about her now. And I'll always wonder where she is and what she's doing. And I'll probably feel guilty once in a while that she's following my example.' I saw the lights of a car on a lonely highway and wondered if that was Rebecca driving off to God-knows-where. 'I still can't quite forgive my parents for choosing to have her the way they did and preferring her to me. But, you know, I do understand now how hard it must have been for her, even if I still think it was harder on me.' I looked up at him.

He had his father's look of amusement, but without the condescension, and with a great deal more warmth. 'It sounds like love, I guess, though a very complicated kind.' His arm went casually around me.

'I think I'd prefer something a little less complicated,' I said, leaning against him and staring up at the vast, star-studded sky.

'Me too,' he replied.

We stayed there until dawn approached. We watched the sunrise feeling as though we were the first man and woman witnessing the dawning of the first day. There, far from the city and all the modern conveniences, it was easy to forget that we were living in a world that had become amazingly, fearfully complex since Creation began.

6

The Beautiful and the Whole

1

I am taking a high-speed train to Paris to meet her. It is not the nearest entry point into Europe from Geneva, where I am staying. But I chose it because for centuries it has been known as the city of lovers. Scientist though I am, I do still have romantic cells in my body. That, thankfully, is something even radioactive or chemical fallout could not kill—the ability of human beings to feel and hope and love, whatever defects their genes may be infected with.

I gaze with interest at the curving titanium and glass ceiling of one of the terminals that I see as I approach the historic Charles de Gaulle airport on the conveyor belt from the train station. Slightly reminiscent of the pyramids bordering the Louvre, this terminal was rebuilt for the second time in the year of my birth, at the end of the last World War. I presume it is designed to cope with vibrations caused by the ultra-supersonic planes that have proliferated in recent years.

Part of it collapsed over a century ago for undetermined reasons. The second time was because of Wartime bombings, of course. It is not the same terminal that collapsed out of the blue, and there has been peace in Europe for a quarter of a century now; still, I feel uneasy.

Part of it is because of the stares headed my way. Europe has been a melting pot of different races for at least four centuries, I know, one of the reasons that precipitated the two World Wars of the first millennium. And certainly Paris, being one of the biggest, loveliest, and most liberal of cities has attracted quite a share of immigrants over the centuries—African, Caribbean, and of course, Filipinos like me, as well as Caucasians from other nations. There are also many blends of these races now due to intermarriage, thus I don't stand out in terms of race, especially in a busy international airport. Should my name be called out, it would not be found terribly unusual, for it sounds like a German-Spanish hybrid: Frankl Veneracion. Not that exotic in Europe, these days. However, the deformities I grew up with, that I have taken for granted so long that it never occurred to me to have any of them repaired even though I can now afford it, these are attracting some attention. My posture is convoluted due to my twisted spine, and I have a missing ear as well as being completely bald. These were the congenital effects of radioactivity and chemicals due to extensive bombing in the War that ended in the year of my birth.

France was bombed as badly as we were. We fought on the same side. But they have risen again in the last two decades following the War, like Northern America and most European nations in the way my own country was never able to. Too many of those left of my country's depleted population absconded to help the world's superpowers to rebuild their war-torn areas, taking advantage of the opportunities for migration offered by more advanced nations such as the one I am in now. I suppose some might think I am one of them, but my cause is scientific and it would have been impossible to pursue it in my Third World country, which has grown pitifully backward since the War. The Philippines seems to have gone back to its pre-colonization era, in the sense of reverting from networks of sprawling cities to small self-contained mountain communities. Many of us even sport tattoos as a badge of honour like members of the old indigenous groups did, though not for the same reasons.

I have always been envious of how most of the First World was able to progress once more following the War, and I am awed at how well Europe has been able to reconstruct many of its centuries-old monuments. Paris is said to be the most exemplary in this regard.

France, like most First World nations, was committed to the improvement of the human race before the War, and they renewed that commitment afterwards, repairing deformities as soon as possible after birth and gathering funds for extensive research on genetics which they have made huge strides in. I know, as I have on many occasions consulted with experts at the Sorbonne for my own work.

I wonder if I should have had myself repaired, to make myself a more presentable bridegroom, dangerous as operations on the spinal cord and inner ear are. Arik, the head of my research unit, has hinted often enough that I could avail of my medical insurance under the university to have any repairs done. Too late now.

I hear her flight being announced, and I hurry as much as my limp will allow it. Then I realize I need not have hurried, for she will still have baggage to collect, customs to go through. I am irritated at having to wait still longer. It was bad enough when I checked the status of her flight when I was getting ready to leave this morning and found it was to be delayed by more than two hours. I seek to contain my impatience. I stand waiting, as erect as I can make myself, propping myself up with my cane like a gentleman in one of those two-centuries-old Impressionist paintings. I stand alert but my mind is far away. For I am remembering the day that I first saw her, twenty-one years ago.

2

I was only four years old then, when I leaned down to peer at little Sabrina, born just days before. She was of course not the first baby I had seen. My own sister had just been born as well—a week ago, prematurely, but I could see her only from a distance, as she was in an incubator and very delicate. The past few months though, I often saw baby Jowendira, a frail solemn thing with withered legs who had been born to the couple living across us. Though she was supposed to be called Wendy, I liked to roll the strange name over my tongue, amused by the jigsaw puzzle her parents put together from her late grandparents' names, Jose, Rowena, Diana, and Rafael, much like my playmate's name Elben was drawn from his late half-sister and brother's names. I often smiled to see the sweet, solemn face of that tiny new descendant of those casualties of War, but neither she nor any baby I saw in childhood, was to strike me as Sabrina did.

My memory of my first sight of Sabrina, though I was just four then, is vivid. I am not certain how much of these were truly lodged in my mind from that age, how much constructed from photographs and other people's memories. It seems the memory grows more vivid as time passes, but is it because I remember more or because my imagination has grown more adept in filling the gaps? I see myself now, a bald-headed, one-eared child peering into a crib at an infant just a few days old. This child is different from the other babies I have seen. Her fair cheeks are rounded and flushed with a hint of rose. There is light brown fuzz all over her head. Still proud of knowing how to count, I count her pearly toes, then her fingers, slowly and carefully out. Ten toes, ten fingers, twenty digits in all. As I finish counting, she grasps my finger and it seems she is looking at me and giving me a smile. Her eyes are bright, her grasp is firm. Her legs kick about slightly. There is no fault in this child. 'She's beautiful,' I gasp.

'And, perhaps more important, she is whole,' murmurs my mother behind me, thinking no doubt of my sister whom she had left at the community clinic, who was missing two fingers, and of my own missing left ear and my twisted spine. The other women who were there with their new-borns told her to be grateful: one was nursing a child missing half his arm, the other watching over a tiny twisted-face baby in an incubator. These women didn't lavish any less love on their babies even with their deformities. But they did worry for them and considered us lucky in comparison.

My mother's arms, holding me up to peer in the crib, begin to tremble—is it from weariness or sadness? She sets me gently on the floor. I reach for my crutch, which is leaning against the crib, but knock it over instead. The clatter wakes up Sabrina's father, a fifty-year-old retired general who had been napping on a couch nearby.

'Get that kid out of here,' Sabrina's grumpy one-armed father roars. He merely grunts at our congratulations. 'My wife was the one who wanted a kid, not me.'

Sabrina's short, dark mother apologizes for her husband as she shows us out. She pats my bald head (I never did grow hair). Mom gives her an understanding smile. After we have gone a little distance from their bungalow, Mom explains that Sabrina's father, General Sison, was injured fighting in the War. But he lost something worse than his arm: he could not find his wife and children when he returned from the War. 'I think he's afraid to love anybody, even his new family, because losing them would hurt too much.'

I do not understand all she says then, of course, though I come to years later. All I am aware of is hearing for the first time of that terrible thing that had happened a few years before I was born, which everyone simply called the War. I ask my mother, 'What is the War? Why were people hurt and lost in it?'

'I'll tell you about it when you are older,' is all she says. 'Now let's go visit your sister in the clinic.'

Not long after, my parents brought home our own baby, my sister Brisa, named for the bracing mountain winds that, my father says, make one glad to be alive. Apart from being very small, and of course, having two stubs instead of ring and little fingers on her left hand, she seemed all right, though she cried a lot, unlike the sweet, gurgling Sabrina. As time progressed, though, Brisa's eyesight worsened so that even as a small child she had to wear thick glasses, without which she was nearly blind. But at least she could look forward to laser surgery when she was an adult. It was a relatively safe procedure for grown-ups, but spinal surgery was another matter. So I had to wear a brace in childhood, even knowing that I could never be completely straightened out. And my missing left ear meant incurable deafness on that side.

Still, my father would never let me feel sorry for myself. 'One thing I learned from that terrible War,' he said, 'perhaps the only positive thing that came out of it, aside from meeting your mother when she was evacuated here, was appreciation for life. Whatever deformities you have, you are alive, and life is precious. That is why I named you Frankl, after the author of a book that helped me find meaning in life again after the War. Whatever little good came out of my sufferings then was not enough, at first, to help me overcome the bitterness over my pain and my losses. But reading that book made me realize I must be grateful for surviving and find a purpose in life, and I found it in my work and in raising my family.'

I was moved and inspired by his story, even as my sister whined about her little defects. It irritated me no end that she made so much of those little flaws when I had to live with much worse. But then she'd always had an unpleasant nature, which was a defect far worse than her physical ones. I tuned her out most of the time and unlike her, listened to my father and let him inspire me with his words and his devotion to science.

I knew something about my father's work as a research chemist, though I was never allowed in his home laboratory. I knew too, because he told me so many times, why he had named me Frankl. But I knew very little about his experiences in the War. They were too terrible to tell, I gathered.

I tried to get others to tell me about this War that had ended just the year I was born. I was the only one among the boys close to my age in our housing complex who could not walk normally. A couple of them were colour-blind, another had ADHD, others had learning disabilities. Karlo was missing his forearm, but he could run around with the rest. They mostly had no patience with my slowness. They were not cruel, being aware of their own deficiencies, but thoughtless and focused on their own pleasure, as children are. Most families had just one computer, which was needed by the grown-ups much of the day for the jobs they tele-commuted to and it could rarely be spared for games or movie-watching. Our childhood, my mother said, was more like that of her great-grandparents than hers, where children barely played outdoors but steeped themselves in electronic activity every chance they got. And generally, it was healthier, but unfortunately, it meant kids like me got left out and had fewer sources of entertainment.

I made the best of things. I figured I had plenty of time to think and wonder while the others played outdoor games. Sometimes I conducted an examination of bugs in the grass. Often, I just sat and pondered.

Sometimes I was joined by Elben, who had a large, black hairy birthmark that covered half his face and the side of his neck. He had the face of a monkey too, and he was often teased by some of the other boys—those with hidden, invisible faults—as looking like a gorilla but, of course, I didn't remark on it. He was able-bodied, big for his age, but he had a problem that grown-ups called dyslexia, which meant he had trouble with reading and was clumsy when it came to throwing and catching and climbing. Even Karlo, who lacked a forearm, was more adept at these activities than him. Whenever Elben found he couldn't keep up with the other boys' activities, he would join me. As we poked about in the grass collecting bugs and stones, we talked, remarking on our parents' recurring laments about the War. We pieced together information we picked up about the War this way.

Later, as my sister grew older, we would play with her and her friends Wendy and Sabrina. My sister Brisa was very much the leader of this little group. Wendy was meek and quiet, in her old-fashioned wheelchair that had to be pushed—her parents didn't work for the government like my father did and hence had few chances to get hold of scarce material resources like a fully-automated 'smart' wheelchair like the kind used by our own Vice-President who had been injured in the war. She had a speech defect as well, and rarely talked to anybody apart from her family and the other two girls. I was a special exception because I had learned out of necessity to lip-read and she only had to shape words with her lips to speak to me. Sabrina was sweet and docile as well, though not exactly submissive. She knew how to make people compromise with her, including stubborn, headstrong Brisa. She sincerely wanted everyone to be happy and had a way of reminding others that such a state was but right.

It was Sabrina who, at the tender age of seven, decided that if we could not get anyone to describe the horrible War, the War which at eleven I started to realize was somehow responsible for the prevalence of birth defects and genetic aberrations, well, instead we would get them to tell stories of life before the War. And so long before it was discussed with us in school, we gained some idea of how the world had changed since the War.

It was hard for us to imagine the world filled with congested cities, living as we did in a typical mountain community that had grown out of a refugee camp, so widely separated from others. The idea of world travel in just days fascinated us too, knowing that now it was very dangerous, seeing that in some nations there was still animosity towards our country or at least our side in the War. Worse, there were still areas that were affected by nuclear fallout and chemicals and even strains of diseases used to fight in the War. Just to go to the murky lowlands in our country, still shrouded in a yellow-green mist, was risky and anyway there was nothing to see there—even if it had been safe to return to the cities, they were too devastated. Not enough people were left, it seemed, to rebuild.

Even little details about those cities thrilled us, like the idea of going into stores filled with toys or books or clothes and just picking out whatever you wanted, buying it and bringing it home. Brand new clothes were a luxury for us, needing to be ordered online and delivered by helicopter to our community. Most of us wore hand-me-downs from our older relatives, mended and altered by the village seamstresses, whose outdated pushbutton sewing machines had been donated by First World countries. Even my sister's glasses were recycled from older children's. We could hardly imagine towns with fountains that weren't meant to give drinking water or to be used for any practical purpose but existed only to be enjoyed. Wasting water for beauty or pleasure was unheard of these days where everything was carefully rationed and regulated due to limited resources. We sighed along with our mothers and longed for the old days.

There were good things, though, we realized, about living in our time. We had seen pictures on the Internet of our country in earlier days, and our mothers described those congested cities as burgeoning with an unruly population and wrapped in an atmosphere polluted with noxious fumes and blaring noise. Our simple town on the mountain sounded idyllic in comparison. More importantly, there might be fewer resources to help people with disabilities now, but at least they were not discriminated against as much anymore. There had been much more staring, more taunts at deformities and aberrations in the old days when the unblemished were the majority rather than the minority, we were told. People were no longer as focused on looks now, at least not the way my mother and Sabrina's mother had been in their teens, going on fad diets, doing chemical treatments on their hair, and begging for cosmetic and plastic surgery treatments. 'People no longer try to look perfect nowadays, and that's just as well,' Sabrina's drab, dumpy mother said, after she and my mother had worn themselves out giggling over how silly and vain they had been in their youth. She looked nothing like her daughter, who was growing more beautiful every day, which made some people wonder if Sabrina's beauty was a genetic aberration after all. Sabrina didn't resemble her sallow, sharp-featured father either.

'Nobody's perfect,' I pointed out.

'In the old days, people would have done a lot to make their children perfect, but it isn't easy nowadays. Not too many good surgeons or prosthetics or such things. Not here, and it's too expensive to go abroad. So it's easier to just accept it,' Mom said.

'I don't know if that's better,' Wendy's mother murmured. She was the youngest of all the mothers, only my age when the war broke out, so perhaps that was why she had not shared much in my mother and Sabrina's mother's experiences struggling with looks. But then she was a naturally beautiful woman, with what my mother called a 'finely-chiselled face,' delectable coffee-and-cream complexion, exotic eyes fringed with thick lashes, and black hair that fell in soft waves. 'I never worried about my looks much until the War broke out. Everyone always told me I was pretty, and I was happy about that. But when it was going on, I was afraid I would get burned in the bombings, or catch one of those horrible disfiguring genetically-modified diseases like leprosy and I would become so ugly that nobody would love me. I couldn't at that time believe that even a parent could love an ugly child. Especially since whenever I mentioned my fears to my parents they would laugh at me and tell me there wasn't any deformity modern medicine couldn't fix, and if anything did happen to me, not that it was likely, they would see to it that it would get fixed. That didn't exactly make me feel better.'

'Of course, you wouldn't know if someone really loved you, unless they loved you even if you couldn't be made perfect,' precocious Sabrina asserted.

The three mothers, resting from the day's chores on a playground bench smiled at her indulgently. Wendy and Brisa just stared at her wordlessly.

'What do you know about it?' Brisa snapped.

We all looked at her in surprise. She was normally quite protective of her friends.

'Well, I just think that you'd really know if someone loved you if they didn't care if you weren't perfect,' Sabrina stammered.

'Maybe, but it still isn't fair!' Brisa stalked off.

My mother went after her. Sabrina's cheeks flushed even pinker than usual, and she burst into tears. Her mother picked her up and carried her home. Wendy's mother turned away and Wendy looked up at me. Her lips formed the words *What's wrong with Brisa?*

It was a strange thing that she didn't think herself referred to in any way by the conversation. Of course, apart from her legs, she looked lovely, having inherited her mother's looks. It was easier for a girl, I thought, since girls preferred quiet games which didn't require running around. 'She's just in a bad mood,' I fibbed. I knew Brisa sometimes tried to see how she looked without her cumbersome glasses but, of course, she could see only a blur in the mirror. She also sometimes asked us why her friends didn't have to wear glasses. The missing fingers bothered her too. She kept her hand in her pocket as much as possible. But they didn't bother her as much as the fact that she didn't have a pretty face like her friends. In vain did my parents try to reassure her that she looked all right even with the glasses. She wanted to look as pretty, if not prettier, than her friends. And, of course, it would have been lying to say she was, with her square face, sallow skin and flat nose.

Little scientist that I was, rather than dwell on my sister's feelings I asked Wendy's mother, 'What's genetically-modified leprosy?'

I learned how long-extinct viruses were revived and made more virulent and contagious by The Enemy. They spread them in the early stages of the War. Most of them were disfiguring and weakening like leprosy and polio rather than deadly, perhaps because they didn't really want to wipe out the citizens yet, just keep them from having the ability and will to fight. 'But it was still terrible,' Wendy's mother said. She was staring off in space, and she seemed to have forgotten she was talking to children. 'My uncle, who was in the military, he had leprosy. His fingers were completely eaten away in just days so he couldn't handle machinery of any sort. He spent the rest of the War quarantined in a hospital. But at least he lived. My grandfather and my aunt got polio. When it came time to flee to the refugee camps, we were asked to leave them behind first. My aunt's legs were completely paralyzed and my grandfather had difficulty breathing. The soldiers who came to take us to the mountains in helicopters said they would send someone for them later but they had to prioritize those who were young and well, those who were likely to survive. A nuclear bomb was dropped before my grandfather and aunt could be taken away from the city.'

It was the first time I'd gotten anyone to tell me anything specific about the War, and I ought to have felt triumphant, but I didn't. I felt horror and revulsion, and wished that I had never asked. When I went to sleep that night, I was haunted by visions of bombs being dropped from the sky, and of leprosy eating away people's limbs. When I woke up, I moved my limbs one by one, to make certain I wasn't paralyzed.

The next day, as I was walking to school, Elben ran up to me, yelling, 'Hey, that was some story, wasn't it, about the War? They should make movies about it.'

'Shut up,' I said, and covered my good ear.

Later that night, I dreamed of being caught in the schoolyard by a bomb, everyone running for cover and leaving me limping to find shelter the best I could. My legs shrivelled up and my ear, my only ear, was being eaten away.

'Wake up, what's the matter?' came my father's voice, and I became aware that I was being roughly shaken. I propped myself up on one elbow, shivering. I was a big boy of eleven, and I wasn't about to cry on my father's shoulder. But he urged me to tell him about my nightmare. Haltingly, I did.

'How could people do such things?' I said.

'I've always asked myself that, Frankl.' He sat down on the bed beside me. 'The countries who used these weapons went on trial after the War. They claimed that these were more humane than radioactive bombs because they disabled rather than killed people.'

'But what they did to people was terrible, almost as bad as killing them.'

He nodded. 'Just pray that this will never happen again. Especially not while our world is still trying to recover from the horrors of that war.'

'What did *you* go through, Dad?' Depressed as I was hearing of the mothers' experiences, I had to ask.

'Too much for you to hear now,' he said. 'Remember, I was working on weapons for the military. Perhaps the worst I went through while there was radiation sickness when the military base was bombed. When I recovered I was pumped full of cancer vaccines and sent home only to be evacuated when the city was bombed.'

'And that's how you ended up here and met Mom?'

'Yes. That's the one bright spot in a terrible event.' He patted my shoulder and stood up. 'You know why I named you Frankl, don't you?' He looked intently at me.

'Yes.'

'Well, make sure you live up to that name. We can't change the past, son, however much we wish we could. But we can do something about the future. Keep that in mind.' He left my room without turning off the light.

And I kept those words in my thoughts as I lay in my small well-lighted room until sleep washed over me again.

3

When I think about it, my life's work began with this knowledge of the War's effects. Another event, two years later, contributed as well. Elben and I were thirteen then and due for genetic testing.

We had no interest in girls yet. Lately, our main interest was going to the library, where pre-War data was being reconstructed and scanned and made available on large-screen computers for those who wished to view it. We perused many pages of 3-D superhero comics together. We talked about what we wanted to do when we grew up. So many jobs seemed alike. Elben couldn't stand the idea of being cooped up indoors like most workers were, whether they worked in data processing or PR. I liked the idea of being a scientist like my dad, but that was as far as I'd worked out my ambitions. Love and marriage didn't figure in dreams of the future yet.

So we thought the whole idea of genetic testing as soon as you reached adolescence was dumb. We told each other so in whispers while we sat in our classroom and waited for our teacher to collect samples of our blood. 'Why not wait until people wanted to get married before they tried to see what genetic defects they might pass on?' Elben wondered, rubbing his birthmark.

Before I could answer, my finger was rubbed briskly with alcohol and pricked. 'Ow!' Everyone in my class received the same treatment from the school nurse. We were then made to line up and sent to the infirmary where we lay down under a body scanner. Then, it was back to schoolwork then PE. Since Elben played soccer and I didn't have a sport, I went home early by myself. We didn't get to talk again for the rest of the day. But I repeated Elben's question to my father at dinner that night.

'It's because they don't want people to get to that point,' my father. 'They can't stop people from getting married if they want to, and they might take the chance even if they knew they could pass something on to their children.'

'It's hard to be logical when you're in love,' my mother said sagely.

'Well, why can't they just keep them from having children?' I demanded.

'It's against human rights, Frankl. Everyone in a democracy has the right to choose whether to have children or not. The most that people can be required to do by the government is to allow themselves to be branded and show the report of their genetic testing to anyone who wants to marry them. The government figures that if they let people know early enough that they aren't fit to have children they'll be resigned to their fate and never entertain thoughts of marriage and children. And it's unlikely anyone will want to marry or have children with those people. After the first few post-War children were born—your generation—people have been fearful of having children the natural way once they saw the defects that were manifested in them.'

'This is true throughout most of the world,' my mother said sadly. 'The entire earth was poisoned by the War.'

'You could get married and not have children,' my sister pointed out.

'The government wants to repopulate the country with healthy citizens. So they want to discourage childless marriages. In any case, it has been proven by history that after a devastating event people are eager not only to marry but to have families.'

'There seems to be a natural instinct to aid repopulation after many losses,' my mother remarked. She smiled up at my father. 'Certainly, we were all too eager to get married only months after we'd met.'

'A lucky thing, since if you'd waited till they passed the genetic testing law, we probably wouldn't have been born,' I said. Despite my defects, I was glad I was alive.

'Why didn't they have genetic testing yet then?' Brisa asked.

'They didn't know how bad it would be till the first generations of post-War kids were born, silly, and aren't you glad or you wouldn't be around,' I said. I bent over my meal, turning my deaf side toward her.

I had spoken without thinking, only wanting to shut her up so I could ask my own questions, but now my own remark gave me pause. Although I could not put the idea into words, I was beginning to sense how any kind of control over reproduction could change a person's destiny, perhaps even the world's.

My father rambled on about genetic testing. 'I suppose it has its benefits. They could do it even earlier, maybe, but I think they want to see first how serious the defects are manifested in the person. They couldn't possibly rule everyone out since, well, nobody's perfect.'

'Does that mean all the children will be perfect?' Brisa asked.

'No, but they're moving in that direction,' Dad explained. 'They want to improve the race, make it a little better than it is now, and hopefully, later they can make it even better and, in the future, it will be like it was before the War and maybe even better.'

'Too bad they never perfected human cloning. That would make it easier, wouldn't it?' I remarked.

'Maybe, but there are too many dangers and complications involved.'

'Not to mention ethics,' Mom added. 'Creating a complete life form, that's playing God.'

'What about the stuff they're trying to do with repairing genes? Isn't that the same kind of thing?' I asked.

'Not really,' Dad said. 'Genes change and improve naturally through evolution. The genetic scientists are merely speeding up and refining the process, much as doctors do when curing diseases. Besides, if there were ever any question about the morality of it before, there isn't now. The genetic damage didn't occur by natural means. Man caused the damage, and now man must repair it.'

Brisa took this opportunity to plead with my parents to have her eyes and fingers repaired. Dad explained to her that it was against the law until she had undergone the mandated genetic testing. Mom started telling her about the expenses and risks. I excused myself and limped off to my room. I sat on my bed and thought about what Dad had said. Dates, marriage, and family all seemed unimportant to me now, but I didn't like the idea that such options would be taken away from me. Still, I knew a lot of other people had worse problems. At least I was only partly deaf, at least I could walk a bit. And what did my lack of hair matter? I wasn't so bad, right?

Wrong. A month after the DNA tests, I got a letter that enraged my father when he read it. 'What's the matter with them?' he roared so loudly that I covered my lone ear. 'The way they talk, you'd think you were stone deaf and bedridden.

How can they say you have two serious impairments when you've always managed just fine?'

'It's all right,' I muttered, embarrassed by the thought that everyone in the neighbourhood could hear him.

'It is not all right, Frankl. You are fit and capable. You say Elben got a positive result?'

'Elben!' Brisa exclaimed. 'Who would want to marry that gorilla?'

I glared at her. 'Yes, they gave him the okay,' I said.

Dad went on, 'Such injustice. Why, you're smarter than Elben. He even has trouble tying his shoelaces.'

'That has nothing to do with brains,' I pointed out.

'Maybe not, but it's important too. We don't live in a primitive society, even if life isn't as easy as it was before the War. Mental ability and skilled fingers are just as important, if not more important in this day and age than mobility and perfect hearing.' He vowed to use some of his connections with government scientists to have the decision reversed.

But nothing came out of it, though my father even went so far as to threaten to sell his research findings to private companies. When the government sent new equipment for his lab, he loaded it back onto the delivery helicopter with a note saying that they weren't going to appease him so easily. Still, the decision seemed final, and I resigned myself to my fate.

Elben and I were branded soon after, I with a dye that showed only in ultraviolet light, like that in our town's singles' disco bar. Elben, like many marriageable types, opted to have his marriageable brand in colour to show off his status. We were all branded but the default was invisible except under ultraviolet light. Elben's rainbow-tattooed mark showed prominently on the cheek that was not covered by his birthmark. He probably figured that with his birthmark, it wouldn't harm his appearance to have a visible imprint on his face. He attended special classes after school on marriage and family life, which he found awfully funny at first but later began to take seriously. He started dating one of the girls who was in the class with him, a talkative girl named Fely who was half his size, being a dwarf.

I spent more time alone, reading material on genetics. My dream was taking shape. I would one day find a way to prevent all birth defects. And then there would be no more discrimination and everyone would feel free to marry and have children.

My interest was nearly obsessive and with all my studying, as my last year of high school drew to a close, I got accepted on scholarship for a foreign university famed for its science program. The letter of acceptance was sent to my school, and I brought it home jubilantly. I couldn't wait to show it to my parents. Surely the occasion justified my calling Dad out of his lab. I dragged myself to our apartment as fast as I could.

As I opened the door, though, I heard something that made me pause. I heard Sabrina's tearful voice. 'I feel so bad, can't you understand?' she was saying.

Brisa replied cattily, 'Well, maybe now you'll see what it's like not to be so perfect.' The next thing I knew, Sabrina was running out the door. She stumbled into my arms and looked up at me in surprise.

Inside our apartment, I heard Brisa squealing, 'Mom, Mom!' She must be looking for our mother to share her news with her. Curious as I was, I could hardly leave. Sabrina was sobbing heartbrokenly and so I just stood there for a while, holding her, looking at her and thinking how beautiful she was. She was thirteen now, though she still looked as she did as a little girl, just a bit taller, and even more lovely. Her smooth honey-coloured hair made a curtain that hid her face. But I could see her in my mind's eye as she was bright-eyed and laughing. She often whispered and giggled with Wendy. With Brisa, it was another matter. I couldn't understand why Sabrina tried so hard to please my sister, who had become even touchier in adolescence. I knew Brisa sometimes tried to coax dimples into her cheeks like Sabrina's and she despaired over her teeth that were now so crooked compared to Sabrina's pearly white ones. She tried different ways of arranging her black hair that was so coarse, not silky like Sabrina's or Wendy's. Nobody could convince her that she looked all right. The only thing that seemed to please her about herself was her figure. She was blossoming while Wendy had only become gangly and Sabrina remained petite and child-like.

'What's wrong? You can tell me,' I said.

'Nothing, only, I dreamed I would get married one day when I was grown up, and now, well, I won't even grow up!' And she flung down a crumpled envelope and ran upstairs to her apartment.

I picked up the envelope which held her test results but decided not to go after her. It would be better to slip it under her door later. I stuffed it in the same pocket where my college acceptance letter resided. I knew it was confidential, so I told myself I wouldn't read it without her permission, just keep it until it seemed the right time to give it back.

I went inside, wondering what mean thing my sister had said to her. I found her in our parents' room with my mother, gloating over the letter which declared her acceptable for marriage and childbearing. 'They say it is all right since I have no impairments that are incurable, or that hinder my ability to perform normal functions,' she explained smugly.

'We're very glad, of course, dear,' Mom said, pretending not to notice I was glowering. Perhaps she thought I was jealous. She seemed unaware of Brisa's cruelty to Sabrina.

'What about your friends?' I asked, trying to keep my tone casual.

'Oh, what would you expect with Wendy? She can barely take care of herself, let alone a baby anyway. And as for Sabrina, they found out something about her. She has something wrong with one of her glands or something like that. Her body won't mature, and she can't have kids! Too bad, isn't it?' But she couldn't hide her elation.

I threw my letter on the bed and lurched out of the room in disgust.

In my room, I took off my shirt, and as I did so, Sabrina's letter fell out of my pocket. I reminded myself of my promise as I picked it up. But Brisa had already told me something of what it said. What else could it say that she hadn't told me? It would simply give me more precise information.

I opened the envelope and drew out the letter. It said something about a benign pituitary tumour, which was suppressing the secretion of glands necessary for her body to mature. The tumour's size and location made it inoperable. She also suffered from other hormonal deficiencies which might or might not be caused by the tumour.

I switched on my slow old computer—a hand-me-down from my father—determined to find out more about the conditions that marked my friend as unmarriageable. But then my family burst into my room full of congratulations.

They tried to dissuade me from going. Why couldn't I do distance education like everyone else? Overseas travel was not as easy as it was before the War; I would not be able to come home for visits. But I made them understand that I had dreams, dreams that would benefit our country and the world, if only I could study what I wished. My father glowed with pride then, and my mother blinked back tears.

Sabrina was not present, being in school. I had told her when I went to give back her letter that I had done my research and found that her condition could be cured by radiation treatment. She merely shuddered. And I understood. Radiation therapy was distrusted by most people who had suffered from the effects of the War. Her mother had often spoken of how she suffered from radiation sickness when she was serving as a military nurse during the War.

I said nothing then, but I vowed to myself I would find a way her condition could be cured. I touched her cheek as I told her I would be leaving to study abroad. To my surprise, she embraced me fiercely.

And so I flew off on the next helicopter, went to the isolated international airport and took off in a plane for the first time in my life. I would not see my family again for four years, after I finished my schooling and returned to my community.

4

Nothing had changed yet everything had changed. The place still looked much the same. Dad was still working for private companies. Elben had started a hydroponic greenhouse. Brisa had graduated and had a boyfriend, a new albino lab technician at the community hospital.

As for Sabrina, I hardly saw her the first couple of days. Then I learned that she spent most of the time in the hospital with her mother, who was dying of cancer. As soon as I could, I extricated myself from my parents and went there. I was led to a room where a woman lay sleeping hooked up to machines and a girl sat bowed over a clunky, old-fashioned electronic book, which fell out of her lap with a thud when I touched her shoulder. She gabbled apologies and congratulations. I took her in my arms.

They had given her mother another month or two, which was about how long I was staying as well. I had little to do, so I came every day to comfort my old friend. Though her body remained prepubescent, her face, lined with sorrow and pain, was a woman's. In an effort to divert her, I even urged her once to go with me to the disco bar, someplace I never even went to myself. Her mother was sleeping peacefully, so she agreed.

We sat at the bar. The bartender looked at Sabrina, whose legs dangled from the stool. 'You're obviously underage,' he said.

I recognized him as a guy who'd been a year ahead of me in school, one of the last victims of the decades-long rage for the souped-up spelling of names that faded with the beginning of the War. Symonn Cayanan, Jr In his time, our school's star basketball player, with his dexterous six-fingered hands. It's a pity he ended up in a job like this. Of course, the area of sports is hardly something our country can afford to develop. In the U.S. he'd probably have earned a scholarship somehow, but he wasn't the brightest student, and most countries give priority to their own. 'Symonn, this is Sabrina. Remember? Well, she was only about twelve when you graduated from high school. But that was years ago.'

'Six years,' said Symonn. He counted it off on one hand, then drummed his fingers, six on each hand, on the bar. 'I must say, you haven't changed.' Sabrina winced. 'So, what will you have?'

'Fortunately, I don't drink alcohol, so you won't get in trouble for appearing to serve it to a shockingly young minor,' said Sabrina. 'Do you have four seasons?' He nodded. I ordered the same.

'It should really be three seasons for me,' she said. It took me a moment to realize she was making a pun on her last name. I smiled, but she grew sober, thinking no doubt that soon there would only be two Sisons. I laid my hand on top of hers.

Around us, the blacklight revealed the tattoos of those invisibly marked, the insignias glowing lavender and indicating whether they were branded marriageable or not. The light also did something for those marriageables with visible tattoos, for their marks were illuminated, giving them an eye-catching glow. The few unmarriageable people stayed on the side-lines in the shadows as much as they could. The marriageables mingled with each other or danced in pairs.

After Symonn served us, we sat sipping our drinks for a while, just watching the people around us. Then I said, 'Would you like to dance?'

'And advertise my unmarriageable status out there? No thanks,' she replied.

'We could probably hide the tattoos if we dance cheek to cheek,' I said, surprising myself with my own words.

Sabrina laughed and said, 'Do they have tattoos in Europe too?'

'Not like ours, as far as I can tell.'

'You mean they have tattoos of different designs or no tattoos at all?'

'I see people with decorative tattoos of all kinds. But as for the status-marking kind, no. As far as I can tell, none at all. Unless they're all invisibly branded like us.'

'Even if they did have them, I guess the design wouldn't be the same,' Sabrina mused. Our tattoo designs were based on the traditional markings of some indigenous tribe that had long died out. 'But, Frankl, how come you don't know? Wouldn't you see them in the disco bars there?'

'Well, I don't go to them. I'm not a nightlife type. I'm a sci-geek, remember? Besides, my university is kind of remote. It's kind of like this town, really. Even quieter, though, as it caters mainly to geeks.'

'Well, but from what I've heard, Europe is a whole different world.'

'Of course, it's different, in many ways. There's snow in winter and everyone skis except me. I can't seem to learn. I can't balance, with my crooked posture. But at least I look almost normal when I'm bundled up in a ski outfit.'

'What do you mean?' Sabrina asked. Then she said, 'Oh. Yeah. I guess I'm so used to you I don't think about your bald head and your ear anymore.'

A slow song came up, and Sabrina slid off her stool. 'I think I would like to dance after all. If you think you can hide this brand on my cheek.'

'Deal. But only if you keep me from losing my balance.'

As we moved out to the dance floor, the lights dimmed and all the invisible tattoos like ours shimmered only faintly. In the near darkness, the issue of status faded to the background, allowing one's true emotions to come to the fore, if only for a moment.

Sabrina's tattoo was barely visible even up close. Still, I held her close, with my tattooed cheek against hers.

It was then that the thought first occurred to me that I could marry her. She couldn't have children anyway. But I felt it was not the right time. She was only eighteen and we would have to part again soon, for I could not do the work I dreamed of in my hometown.

Before I left, we spent a few more weeks of quiet companionship. There were days when we hardly said anything to each other, but the silence was never awkward. I would sit reading research updates. Sabrina took up digi-knitting and would tap out designs on the touch-screen of a small machine, from which emerged a neat ski cap that she presented me with the day before I left. I hugged her, unable to speak, wary of revealing what was growing in my heart.

I returned to my university to work with a team that was developing cancer vaccines. It sounds like a rather old-fashioned field of study, but isn't really, since cancer has been evolving along with the human race, growing in complexity and making itself even harder to defeat. It has developed in various patterns in different countries, depending on what chemical, genetic or radioactive weapon attacks they received during the War. My work was absorbing and my days were filled with little else besides. My nights were spent in a lonely dormitory room, chatting over the Internet with family and friends. Especially Sabrina.

With only her face to view on my monitor, it was easy to stop thinking of her as a child. She was getting a college degree in something called global cultural studies through distance education but in her spare moments, she chatted with me. She fended off my questions about her life after her mother's death, bugging me instead to tell her about my surroundings, which I must confess I hardly ever noticed anymore. For her sake, I sought to notice and remember more. The poor girl was feeling trapped, I realized, and sought vicarious freedom in hearing about my routine days.

The next time I returned home was two years later, for Elben and Fely's wedding. It was a simple affair, like most weddings are in my country, at least since the War. The reception was a gathering of old friends in Elben's hydroponic greenhouse. Having lettuce as hanging plants does not sound very romantic, even if it is the ruffled variety. And the only flowers were squash blossoms. But though it could not rival the lavish weddings of my mother's older siblings, God rest their souls, that I have seen in her precious digital albums of photos, well, I'd say it was just as happy. And romantic. Even for me.

Brisa was invited but refused to come, sulking because Elben hadn't invited her boyfriend too; Wendy wasn't around, as she had a hands-on training session in her course in librarianship, and the rest of the guests were all Elben's old soccer teammates and Fely's friends.

And Sabrina. I saw her slip into the church as I was standing in front as best man. I smiled to see her looking so small in her dress, long with flowing sleeves to her wrists, clattering in like a child trying on her mother's high heels. We didn't get to talk at all at the wedding, but we found ourselves standing next to each other as we prepare to pelt the newlyweds with flowers. In the day of my late uncles and aunts, Mom tells me, rose petals were the fashion, colour-coordinated with the wedding as genetically modified blooms could be ordered in any shade—purple was especially popular the last few years, she said, which I find odd. Anyway, that would be incredibly extravagant these days. And to go back to earlier times and use rice would be even more shocking, with our community's horror of food waste. Instead, we fling handfuls of tiny sampaguita buds.

As we entered Elben's greenhouse for the reception, Sabrina took my arm. She asked me a few questions about my life abroad, then as we approached the reception table, we fell into a bemused silence along with the other guests. The long table held nothing but a white tiered cake decorated by a length of blossoming squash vine, a punch bowl, platters of bread and cheese, and bowls of salad dressing. There was also a pile of plates at one end and a pile of colanders at the other. Elben, the merry bridegroom, handed around the colanders, inviting us to 'Go wild among the vegetables!' We were to pluck our own ingredients for salad, rinse them and toss them with dressing. A fountain had been set up in the centre for washing them.

I took mine and gazed at the greenery around me. 'I have to say, I may be a biologist but I don't know a thing about botany. Are those grapes?' I pointed to some vines hanging with small green and orange fruits.

Sabrina was in hysterics. 'Those are cherry tomatoes!' She plucked a red one and handed it to me; tasting it, I saw she was right.

'I suppose you were thinking of the vineyards in Europe,' she remarked.

'I've never seen one, to tell you the truth. There never were any near the places I've stayed. And I'm not much for sightseeing. I've never set foot in a museum, though there are hundreds over there and everyone goes to them, not just art geeks. The only art I've seen is in university buildings and in colleagues' homes.'

'Frankl,' she said in exasperation. 'You had a chance most of us never hoped to have, to not only study abroad but to see something of the world. And you don't even want to see it!' She filled her colander with tiny tomatoes and variegated lettuce.

'It might be different,' I said, 'if you were with me.' I gathered some squash blossoms and held them out to her. 'I'm leaving in ten days. Will you come with me?'

'I can't. My father would never allow me. I'm all he has left. I just hope you'll take some time to enjoy the scenery from now on. You can tell me all about it, share some photos, maybe.' She tossed the squash blossoms among the greens and tomatoes in her colander. 'Anyway, it wouldn't look right, me going abroad to stay with you.'

It was my turn to be exasperated—unreasonably, I admit. I grabbed her arm and pulled her roughly to me. She flinched and I winced, thinking what it meant, what she must be enduring at her father's hands—hand. 'Sorry,' I whispered. I cupped her face gently. 'Sabrina, I'm asking you to marry me.'

She stared at me steadily. 'You know how it is at a wedding,' she said in her sage child's voice. 'Everyone wishes they were the bride or the groom.'

'But I'm sure. I love you. I know I'm not much to look at, but I love you.'

She blinked and lowered her eyes. 'I've never cared how you looked. I've always loved you. But are you sure?'

There was only one answer to that. I drew her in my arms and there, among the tomato vines, I kissed her. When she spoke again, her voice was trembling. 'Oh, Frankl. You know my father would never consent. And whatever he does, I don't want to hurt him. Will you wait one more year?'

It was on the tip of my tongue to tell her she owed her father nothing, but I remembered what my mother had said about his past, and tried to understand. 'I will wait a year until you come of age. And, if you must, bring him too,' I told her. 'Just come to me.'

She answered with a smile and a swift kiss.

5

For the year that followed, all our communications were online. A year of sharing our dearest hopes over a screen and a year without a single kiss. Longing to hold her in my arms overwhelms me and impatiently I shift and look about for her again.

While I was lost in my reverie, waves of passengers had issued forth, torqueing around me where I stand. But I see no Sabrina. Could we have somehow missed each other? I stump to the information desk. The trim young woman behind the counter speaks to her computer, asking for the passenger manifest of Sabrina's flight. 'Yes, here she is. Miss Sison boarded at Subic Bay International Airport on the date you gave. Direct flight, no stopover.'

'So why isn't she here? Did she get off the plane at all? Did she go through customs or not?'

She looks confused. 'I have given you the information you requested, sir. If it is somehow incorrect, perhaps there is an inefficiency at the airport where she boarded.'

All sorts of possibilities flit through my mind. Could there be a different passenger with the same name? But no, that was the flight number of the ticket I purchased online for her. Could she have changed her mind last minute after handing in her boarding pass and just run off? The airline probably wouldn't allow her to leave just like that. If this was a totalitarian nation, then I might suspect she was whisked away by a customs official for something she was carrying that appeared suspicious but was actually innocuous or if someone tried to pass drugs or something through her luggage. Surely they wouldn't do something so underhanded here. I demand to see someone who can help me unravel this mystery.

'But what else can be done, sir?'

'Something can always be done. Call somebody else. Your superior, the customs official, somebody who knows more.' I pound my fist into the counter.

The woman speaks into the mouthpiece of her headset. Moments later a man arrives, a grim official-looking person in a dark suit. I wonder if she died on board, maybe under mysterious circumstances and they have to keep it confidential. But the man only says, 'There is no such person as the one you are looking for. Not on this plane. No doubt she never boarded at all.'

'But we just saw her name on the screen.' I point to the passenger manifest on the monitor. We all look at it. But now Sabrina's name is not visible on the screen.

'There may be a misunderstanding or mistake, but that is nothing to do with us, sir, I assure you. I must ask that you leave now, Mr Veneracion.'

I start to protest, then decide it is futile to remain here. I had an appointment at the consulate, reservations in Paris, and tickets for the regular train, the one that went slowly through the countryside and was favoured by tourists. But that was all for Sabrina's sake. Now I simply leave the Charles de Gaulle airport, stumble back to the station I came from, and take a high-speed train straight back to Geneva.

I cannot believe this is happening. We had planned our wedding down to every last detail before I left home. We had lain on a grassy slope the night before I left to talk about our hopes after watching the last remake of the movie whose eponymous character she had been named for: *Sabrina*.

This version was made at the beginning of the War and was thus full of subtle references to the possibility of disaster while still being innocently hopeful. The character Sabrina was studying abroad when she witnessed a frightening bombing. This near-death experience made her determined to win the man she loved. When she returned to the mansion where her father was a chauffeur, she saw the two brothers who lived there—the older myopic and with a slight limp unfit to fight in the War and the younger that she loved who shut his eyes to the brewing conflict. She won him over but ultimately grew more interested in the older brother who was trying to break up their relationship so his brother would focus on the family business. Later, the younger brother volunteered to fight in the War and everyone realized that Sabrina had more to contribute to the family business. And that she and the older brother had fallen in love.

The couple reminded us so much of ourselves we couldn't help but be in a romantic mood after the film ended. We wandered off on our own, hand in hand. It was the night of a meteor shower and the magic of the sky filled with shooting stars made everything seem possible. We talked about our future together. We would visit all the most romantic cities in Europe, at least those that were not currently undergoing restoration, starting with Paris. We would shop for her wedding bouquet at the famous Marché aux Fleurs, another sight I had never seen but that she knew about through her research. She described the vast market of flowers near the Notre Dame as if she had been there herself. We would visit the famous cathedral too, of course, an appropriate place for me, I joked, given that I was nearly a hunchback. We would tour Italy, then back in Geneva we would rent a Swiss chalet near the university instead of staying at the dormitory.

As a shower of meteors filled the sky, I told her to make a wish and she grew pensive. When our conversation about our wedding resumed, she was sombre. She asked me about the possibility of a normal married life. With children.

I told her again that her condition might be curable with radiation therapy. That was perhaps her only chance as of now. Laser surgery was not powerful or accurate enough to excise her tumour. I told her this.

She chewed her lip. 'Isn't there a risk I'll get cancer from radiation therapy?'

I nodded. 'It's possible, yes.'

'You're developing vaccines for these cancers, aren't you?'

'Yes. Of course, there are already vaccinations for some cancers. But not all.' I explained to her how difficult the study of cancer was with those who had been born during and shortly after the War. Such a variety of environmental factors had affected us, from radiation to genetically modified microbes, that cancer in those of our generation could be quite volatile and manifest itself in surprising ways. At the same time, probably since we were not that old, not enough of us had developed cancer yet for its manifestations in our population to be acutely studied. Cancer is such a tricky thing, mutating itself even as we mutate. Currently, it appears most of the cancer vaccines developed before the War have not been very effective to those of us born during and right after it.

'Suppose, Frankl,' Sabrina said, 'Suppose that you were able to vaccinate me from all the cancers it could cause. Or say, even, that I was willing to take a risk.'

'I wouldn't want you too. And the fact is, I'm not sure I want children at all. Not that I don't like them, but . . .'

The truth was that the main problem was me. I could pass my myriad genetic defects on to my offspring. Actually, so could my sister, but our illogical government doesn't seem to have worked that out. I suppose the logic in branding me unfit for reproduction is that there's a stronger chance of the dominant genes being passed on. And in any case, Brisa could do what she wanted, but I had my own principles and I saw the logic of the laws deterring me from reproducing. I didn't want to be responsible for bringing severely disadvantaged children into the world.

I found myself unable to say this, but Sabrina clearly sensed some of what was going through my mind. She took my hand and said, 'It's all right.' I kissed her deeply with a mix of gratitude and regret.

Remembering this, I wonder if she could have changed her mind about me. That would have been reason enough. But why not tell me? Why disappear in this way? There must be some other explanation.

I arrive in Geneva and hurry to the university. Upon entering my dorm unit, I insert my key card into a slot by the door, turning on everything in my room, including my computer. 'Mom! Dad!' I yell, approaching it. The screen blinks on, split in two, one side showing each of my parents.

Dad, working in his lab, peers over his glasses and says sternly, as is his habit, 'Is this an emergency, Frankl?'

Mom, combing her hair in the bedroom, doesn't ask. I can see in her eyes she intuitively knows it is and excuses herself to cancel her videoconference with her editorial staff, blinking off then reappearing on my screen.

My parents tell me that she came to tell them she was leaving the night before, that she had seemed sure despite her father's disapproval. And they gave her a package to deliver.

'What?' I groaned. Could that have been her undoing? 'No reports of your secret projects or anything like that, Dad?'

'I wouldn't do that, son, and I have no European clients now, in any case. It was your mother who chose the things, a wedding present, some things she thought you might be able to use.'

Mom tells me to try to relax, that she will call the local airport herself since I was clearly too distraught to deal with anyone now. 'But first, I'll run up and talk to Sabrina's father.'

I call Brisa, who is annoyed at being disturbed and says that she doesn't know anything, then Wendy, who is in the library digitally tagging recent news articles. I turn up the volume on my computer to hear her better. 'Sabrina didn't tell me anything but goodbye,' she says. 'But wait. What is her flight? There is something here about a plane that made an unexpected stopover for inspection by the military, who had information about a possible bomb on board.'

I give the flight number. It is the same. That explains the close to three hours delay. 'Where?' I ask. She names a totalitarian state in Eastern Europe.

I call the airport in that country. They give me no information other than what Wendy gave me. 'Did any of the passengers leave the plane?'

'Of course. They had to be evacuated in order to make a thorough search. But they were contained in one area and reboarded after.'

'All of them?'

'I'm certain, sir.'

'Could anyone have left?'

'That would have been impossible. The passengers were under heavy guard as they were all suspects. The entire affair was handled by the military. We do not take bomb threats lightly.'

'But you found no bomb?'

'No, sir.'

'And you checked that all the passengers reboarded. All of them?'

The mildly accented voice hesitates. 'That is the responsibility of the airline, sir.'

It all came back to that. Sabrina's father reported that he had seen his daughter off. He had walked her to the helipad, he said. 'That was kind of him, considering he is a semi-invalid,' Mom remarks. Also uncharacteristic of him, I think, given how mean and disapproving he is.

The airline also reported no passenger of the name. 'Could she have taken another flight?' I ask Mom.

'I thought of that,' Mom replies. 'I asked them to check the manifests of all the flights on that day. Nothing.'

So it seems only one other possibility remains. That she had gone to the airport and decided not to take that flight. That she had changed her mind about marrying me and gone to live in some other community rather than go back to her father. That she was now living somewhere else, ashamed to talk to me.

'Thanks, Mom, and goodbye,' I said. 'Goodbye, Dad. I'm going now.' The screen turns black. Then, I think of something. I call, 'Sabrina. Sabrina!'

The screen remains black.

6

There is nothing left for me to do but continue with my research on cancer vaccines. My colleagues are surprised to find me back on Monday, as I had requested a week's leave. Thankfully, I had been a bit embarrassed to give the real reason, merely saying I was escorting a visiting family friend on a tour of Paris. To be sure, I had Sabrina's picture on my computer screen, but photos of my family and other friends appear as well. Only my boss Arik has remarked on Sabrina, but I never felt close enough to him to tell him about my engagement. Somehow, I never could tell anyone at work. And nobody seems to have made the presumption that she was my fiancée. Probably because they couldn't believe it of me, with all my defects.

Of course, we sci-geeks tend to be not that romantically inclined. As far as I know about the others in the lab, only the British-Indian Sanj is engaged, and that was by family arrangement. Jac and Cristofer are good-looking enough, it seems to me. None of them have obvious defects like me, but they don't go on dates very much. I guess it's not something most of us single-minded scientific types think about much.

I have to admit I'd been secretive about our relationship. The fact was, I could never quite believe that we really would get married. I always had a sense of foreboding that something would prevent it. Well, as it turns out it seems as if we really aren't meant to be together. This is a ridiculous, unscientific thought, but in the depths of my depression, I am unable to shake it.

Arik remarks on my industriousness; after all, having been granted the leave I could simply have gone on holiday on my own. I reply briefly that I didn't want to go anywhere alone. Margret, who acts motherly to me though she's mere months older, asks me if something is wrong, but I just bend over a microscope and tell her that my friend had a change of plan, that I was disappointed I wasn't going to see my friend anymore, but well, what could I do.

Then, before the week ends, I see her.

It is my habit to wake early and take my time climbing up the hill to the building where I perform my research, as my body is painfully stiff in the cool morning air. This morning, I am the only one about when I leave the building. I don't blame the others for taking their time. There is an unseasonable chill in the air, reflecting the chill in my heart. I pull my ski cap, the one Sabrina made for me, down over my ear. I am still consumed with puzzlement and frustration over her disappearance, but I have run out of ideas on what to do.

As usual, I find it easier to take a winding road passing behind the buildings than the steeper direct path. I suppose I ought to get a scooter or car, but to one who has grown up used to doing without, that seems like an extravagance.

I don't even have a cell phone, though I certainly can afford that. The lab provides us with tablets, but I keep mine locked in my desk drawer after work, fearful of losing what to me is an expensive luxury item. There was no point in having portable communication devices in the small community I grew up in, and my circle of acquaintance here in Europe is limited to those I see every day.

As I approach the parking lot behind my building, the back door opens and out comes Arik, leading a girl who is rolling her sleeve down over her bandaged arm. The wind lifts her honey-coloured hair, just for a moment, but long enough for me to recognize her for certain.

'Sabrina!' I shout, limping faster toward her, as fast as I am able. She looks at me; so does Arik, then he turns, dragging her quickly to a car and shoving her in.

'Arik!' I roar. I stumble forward, tripping over my feet. For the first time in many years, I curse my disability, my slowness, and even my lack of a cell phone. The car drives off and Arik returns to the building before I can even set foot in the parking lot.

I spend the day in the lab doing my work and pondering over the meaning of these events. I don't see Arik till the afternoon, when he comes in with a bottle of champagne and orders everyone to gather around him. Smiling, he says, 'I have an announcement. A private organization is giving us additional funding for our research.' With that, he uncorks the bottle and calls for glasses. People cheer and hold out mugs and laboratory flasks. They buzz around him with questions: How much (it's sizeable)? What organization (it's confidential)?

I watch him and take no champagne. How smooth, how cool he is. Quite suave for a sci-geek. I almost doubt what I had seen this morning. But I could not possibly have imagined it since I never would have made any connection between Arik and Sabrina.

As people drain their glasses around me, I suddenly say, 'I have an announcement too.' The room continues to buzz. I raise my voice, saying, 'I would like to announce my resignation.'

Silence. Everyone looks at me.

'You can't quit now!' Jac says. He is echoed by the others.

Arik stares back at me impassively and smooths down the front of his crisp black jacket. 'Well, we will certainly miss you, Frankl,' he says, with a faint, false smile. 'But it is your choice, of course.'

I get together my things. 'You're leaving now?' Sanj asks. He and the other lab assistants follow me outside. I hug Margret and slap the backs of the guys. Of course, they want to know why I'm leaving but I'm deliberately vague.

'A new job?' asks Margret. 'I hope it's a high-paying one. Then maybe you can get yourself fixed up and find a nice girl.'

I just look at her and she says, 'I'm sorry if I offended you. I didn't intend to be rude. Most of us who were born during and after the War needed some fixing up too, you know. Remember, it's covered by insurance here so it's done as early as possible. Just essential things, of course. I had a cleft palate, but I always wished they'd done something about my crooked nose while they were at it. And it didn't keep me from becoming overweight!'

Sanj says, 'It has caused a problem though, for many Indian families. They have to investigate to find out a prospective mate's original defects.'

'What's yours?' the others ask.

'My heart. It was rather serious. Fortunately, there was a compatible transplant of the right size available in the deep freeze.' In a low voice, he adds, 'Not all of the War's victims died in vain.'

'Good thing they found a girl for you, though,' Margret remarks.

'Yes, and she is perfect, all but a missing kidney. Her family chose me because my father is a specialist in kidney disease, which makes up for the fact that I was born with a serious defect.'

'Well, I have a fake nose,' Jac says. We make sounds of disbelief and he protests, 'No, really, I do. Want me to take it off and show you?'

'No thanks!' Margret retorts.

'Just kidding. I'm a few years older than you lot, so I was a toddler during the War. Got a bit affected by a genetic bomb which ruined my skin and ate away my nose. Really, it did. But it was all fixed later. Doesn't come off though. Got you there.'

'Transplanted cartilage?' I guess.

'Yes. They could do that with your ear, Frankl.'

'What for? That would hardly make a dent in all my defects,' I say.

'Guess what mine is,' Cristofer says. We stare at him. Before any of us can answer, he grabs my hand. 'Feel this!' he says, placing it on his thigh. I'm embarrassed, wondering what he means by this when I realize that his thigh is rigid. 'The leg on the other side is like that too,' he says.

'Not to mention the one in the middle,' Jac quips, and everyone laughs.

I don't feel like laughing but I manage a smile. Even in my anxiety, I am surprised how at ease I feel with this international group of scientists. Of course, with my German first name and Spanish last name, I could come from anywhere.

I repeat my goodbyes, then I tell them all, 'Keep in touch. If anything . . . peculiar . . . seems to be going on here, let me know, okay?'

My friends are puzzled but promise anyway.

I take a high-speed train to Eastern Europe, scanning science job sites on my computer on the way. I send applications to several places, arranging for interviews the very next day. I don't know what I am looking for exactly, but I have a hunch I will find a clue in the country where Sabrina's plane was detained.

Just as there have been neo-Nazis, there have been neo-Socialists, and these have taken over several Eastern European countries. Not as many as in the previous millennium, to be sure. The neo-Socialists took over soon after the War and have remained in power. The name of their federation was always a joke to us, back in school. Soviet Union of Socialist States. SUSS. We would exclaim whenever it came up in a discussion, 'Ay, SUSS!' The English equivalent of this pun was 'Gee, SUSS!'

Well, I soon find the actual life here is nothing to laugh about. There is an air of dreariness in these countries, it seems to me, though perhaps it is just the chilly weather. I don't have much choice about my housing, which is assigned to me by the lab that hired me, but I soon find that it is no different from the housing of other single men. I learn this as over the next two years, I move from one institute to the other and have to move to new assigned housing, usually a drab studio apartment, each time. Well, the better to cover my tracks.

The more densely populated areas usually require shared rooming for singles, and one has no choice of roommates either. It doesn't matter much to me who I room with, in any case, since I am too absorbed in my quest and move too often to take an interest in the person I'm boarding with.

Although it hurts my credentials, I never mention my previous laboratory experience, only my education, fobbing off the year after graduation to assistance to my father in some private research. I work on everything from cloning endangered species to testing fertility drugs. I try to meet as many people as I can in the scientific community. I ponder the military connection as well. It is a military state, so they are everywhere.

My search is going nowhere when I am called home. My father is undergoing surgery to remove some tumours. I decide while I am there to confront Sabrina's father, something I should have done in the first place.

After my father's operation, when he is safely recovering, I leave my family and go barge in on Sabrina's father. He is alone. Sabrina told me that she contracted a nurse to stay with him the week she left, but he must have dismissed her. Maybe he never paid her. I could believe almost anything of this unnaturally cold man. He does not look the least bit startled by my bursting in and demanding, 'What have you done with her?'

'What are you talking about?' the old man says, raising one intimidating eyebrow.

I lay forth my theory. That he had allowed the military to abduct Sabrina when her plane was detained. That he had sold her to a foreign government for some cruel experiment. Something to do with cancer. Though why they wanted her, I couldn't understand. Did it have to do with her beauty and perfection? Did they wish to test potentially cancer-causing chemicals on her?

'You're supposed to be the genius, boy,' General Sison says. 'I don't know a thing. Do you really think I wanted to lose my unpaid housekeeper and nurse?'

'You might have been willing to, for a profit.'

'I don't look like I've profited, do I?' He laughs. 'Look at the way I live. I'm flattered that you think my position in the military could get me anywhere with the foreign powers when I couldn't even get a decent prosthetic arm from them. So what if they were our allies? They were the ones who declared War in the first place and drafted our assistance. Then, once the War was over and they no longer needed our manpower, did they do anything for us at all? Their excuse was that they needed all their funds to rebuild their own nations. They argued that it was enough that they dumped their old technology on us in the form of donations. There's gratitude for you. We didn't have to get in the War if it hadn't been for them.'

I ignore his rants and persist in questioning him. 'So you're saying you know nothing? That you have no power, no power at all?'

The old man's pride must have been riled by that, for he bristles and says, 'I know nothing of what you're talking about, but I do have some power, some connections. Tell me what you need. I have enough friends in high places and I can get you favours.'

Is it possible he's telling the truth? I stare at him. 'I'll let you know if I need anything.'

I decide to take a chance and trust him. I have nothing to lose. But what do I ask for? What is the key? I lie awake all night, thinking. Finally, I hit upon something and first thing in the morning I rush over to tell him. The only definite clue I have is Arik. Shall I have him exploit Swiss connections and have Arik captured and questioned?

When I tell him this the next day, he laughs at my suggestion. 'I don't have quite enough power for that. No, I can't do that. But since you know the person and the date, then it should be a cinch for a hacker.'

We work out a strategy. He puts me in touch with a military intelligence agent he knows, an excellent hacker. We will try to find the archives of Arik's correspondence with this mysterious private company. Or it might be with the military of that country. It's possible.

I'm surprised when I see the hacker online. Evalene could be my mother, being about the same age. But she's the ultimate 'puter-geek', as she calls herself, with a smile. She insists that I call her Evalene. Just Evalene, surname withheld. I hesitate at first, avoiding calling her anything initially, then call her Evalene since she corrects me each time I call her Ma'am. I also feel somewhat wary about sharing the details of my quest with her when I'd kept them secret even from my family. As we discuss the case, I eventually feel at ease with calling her by her first name and with confiding everything. She questions me briskly and I tell her everything I can.

The date is easily narrowed down. I only made the online purchase of Sabrina's ticket two weeks before her twenty-first birthday. She only spoke to her father about her decision at that time; it made more sense than spending a year living with his ire.

'Who else knew?' Evalene asks me. 'We have to search every possible connection.'

But there was nobody else, except my parents, of course. I didn't dare announce it to too many people for fear she might change her mind at the last minute. I did apply to Arik for leave the minute Sabrina confirmed she was coming. Was that enough to tip him off? How would he know about her, anyway? I never talked much about her to him. I've never been one to chat about my personal life. And I don't get drunk either. But suppose I revealed more than I realized. Did he suspect she was the friend I was going to meet in Paris, and alert his connections?

We stick to Arik. Most of his communications are scientific in nature, most are about our cancer vaccine project to private firms he applied to funding for. 'I think we're looking for something to do with the military,' I tell Evalene.

'There doesn't seem to be anything to do with the military at all. But if it's the military, their security is sure to be higher, and it will take longer to breakthrough. Not impossible, just more difficult.'

'I've been searching for two years,' I tell her. 'I don't care how long it takes.'

'There's some personal correspondence here. Something about a fishing trip. And a lot of discussion with a man about M-16s. Your boss appears to be a vintage gun buff.'

'I didn't know much about him,' I admit.

'Some other personal correspondence, to a woman, about whether she wants a daughter. That was just the day you were supposed to meet Sabrina. And that's it. No more.'

'No military correspondence?'

'If there is, it's possible an alias was used. Go through the material I hacked for you again and see if there's any hint of something unusual.'

I go through them all day, impatiently scanning form letters, applications for grants that give the details of our research which I know very well. Not a clue in the correspondence itself. Still, I note the names of the addressees, all heads of private firms. There is a more detailed version using more technical language, to a guy named Mihalovich, head of a private lab, it appears. I go through the personal correspondence. The name Mihalovich crops up again, in letters about M-16s. Did they belong to some club of gun collectors? For there is a reference to an M-16 to be sent to Charles. Arik advises Mihalovich to intercept it and deliver it to him for preparation.

And then it hits me. I don't deserve to be called a genius. How could it have taken me so long? I conduct a search on Mihalovich. There are dozens of scientists named Mihalovich in the world, but I stick to those in Eastern Europe. My stumbling block is that there is little that is translated into English, and often the translations are badly done. I decide to go to the library, hurrying to get there before it closes.

Once there, I make my way to the journal section. I look up all the Mihalovichs and skim through their articles. There is a Mihalovich who was the director of a hospital's cancer research division in the U.S. I'm pretty sure that is the one and search for more information on him. I find that the man died three years ago.

I find myself going through the pre-War print journal articles as well. There is a Mihalovich who just graduated before the War, awarded for his thesis on gene reconstruction. His paper is reproduced in a journal. But if he was such a hot-shot scientist, how come there are no other reports of his research afterwards? Was he killed in the War?

'Excuse me, sir, it's closing time,' the head librarian says to me.

'I'll take care of closing up, sir,' interjects a familiar voice. Familiar, but stronger. It is Wendy, looking very much at home in the library. 'Doing some important scientific research, I suppose?' she says.

'Something like that.' I don't confide the reason for it, but I do tell her what I'm looking for, and she helps, her fingers flying expertly over the screen to find what I want. We find out more about this Mihalovich in the news archives. He is awarded for his work on genetic weaponry during the War. Top secret stuff, which explains there was nothing about him between then and his graduation. Then later there is news about him receiving grants and awards, then heading a government-sponsored population regeneration project. This is followed by a number of articles by him that read like PR, urging people to donate their sperm and eggs to the project, promoting in vitro over natural reproduction as a way of improving the race. 'In vitro fertilization is better, more controlled. We can analyze the embryos and select those with minimal defects to be implanted,' he says. He doesn't say what is done with the others.

I am beginning to form my suspicions about this man when I find a headline about his being fired by the government. He had been harvesting extra sperm and eggs to use for illegal experiments. He justified himself by saying that he needed to do many trials to find means of eliminating various birth defects. He explained this necessitated creating hundreds of test-tube babies with controlled genetic combinations. That meant combining the extra sperm and eggs to his liking, without the permission of the donors A few people sympathized with him but most agreed with the government's action. Not surprisingly, there is nothing more about this Mihalovich after that.

I stare silently at the news photo of the man, about forty at the time judging from his appearance and his hairline which is starting to recede.

'Do you know this man, Frankl?' Wendy asks.

'Not personally,' I don't explain further.

'It's amazing how many illegal activities have grown around in vitro fertilization,' Wendy remarks. 'I've read a lot of news items about sperm trafficking and egg trafficking, where they kidnap people and force them to donate. Though those stories mostly date back to when we were in high school. I don't see them in the current news so much.'

I mull over that. 'It isn't that common anymore, I suppose, since genetic scanning is common now. I'm sure people ask to see the microscans of the donated material. They'd have to get someone who is just about perfect to pass muster. And that would be hard.' I pat her shoulder and snatch up my cane. 'I think I'm done here. Thank you.' And I stumble out the door.

Egg trafficking. That must be it. But how am I supposed to find an illegal outfit? I contact Evalene and ask her to mine Mihalovich's internet activity. Then I return to my family in the hospital.

My father is quite well, though not strong enough to talk much. I decide it's better not to tell them about the latest developments in my search just now, knowing how excitable he is.

Brisa is there, too, of course. She is actually happy to spend her entire day at the hospital since her lab technician boyfriend can drop by and see her often. While we sit at Dad's bedside together, she plies me with questions about my work and travel, and I answer vaguely.

'Meet any new women?' she asks. 'Not that any marriageable one would want to go with you.' She tosses back her hair on the side where the bright blue tattoo that marks her as a marriageable glows on her cheek.

'I had my chance,' I say. 'It wasn't my fault it didn't work out.'

'Yeah, well, forget about her. She was just using you to get to go abroad, clearly. You're not still hoping to see her again, are you?'

I say nothing.

'Can you honestly say you really loved her? I mean, would you have loved her if she wasn't beautiful and whole?'

I am furious with her for making me doubt my own feelings. Of course, I loved—love her. Her beauty, well, that was part of who she was. It wasn't the real reason I loved her. I would love her even if I found her horribly disfigured and deformed. I'm sure of it. Of course, I am. All I need is to find her so I can prove how much I love her.

'I will find her,' I tell Brisa. 'I am returning to Eastern Europe. I know I'll find her there.'

'How do you know, genius?' she sniffs.

'Because I won't give up until I do.'

<h1 style="text-align:center">7</h1>

When I get the information from Evalene, I set to work. I create a new identity for myself. I am Victor Gallo, a Eurasian from Hong Kong seeking to have a clone child, one who will be guaranteed to be free of all my genetic defects. I order a prosthetic ear and a brown wig for the purpose, to be delivered to my European address. I suppose I can trust my roommate to receive them for me though I barely know him since as a medical intern he keeps such poisonous hours we rarely see each other. I can think of no way to disguise my crooked body; anyway, I can easily explain it away since spinal surgery is known to be risky.

I stop at my apartment long enough to pick up my packages. Then I ride my scooter to Mihalovich's lab. It is a long ride, to a rural area. Thank heavens for solar-powered scooters, or I would have run out of gas. The place does not look like a lab as such but an out-of-the-way farmhouse. I am ready to meet him, disguised and with the name of one of his old clients that Evalene sourced for me as a reference.

Mihalovich is older than in the pictures of him I've seen, yet his hairline seems to have grown back rather than receded farther. He greets me warmly, asks how I found out about his 'clinic' as he calls it. Then he gets down to business.

'Yes, we have superior cloned embryos here. Do you have a male or female child in mind?'

I am careful not to seem obvious and simply shrug. 'It doesn't matter as long as the child is healthy. Can you guarantee that?'

'Of course, Mr Gallo.'

'How?'

'Our lab is meticulous in analyzing the genetic material. If you decide to work with us, we will give you all the genetic data. Surely you must know that. You came all this way.'

'Just making sure,' I mutter.

He leans forward and fixes his gaze on me. 'But tell me, are you married? Or have a, as they say, life partner?'

'Of course,' I lie. 'I just wanted to find out more first, so I can convince my partner to go into this. If we decide it's for us.'

'I would think your partner would have more stake in this since I presume she is to bear the child. Can you tell me more about your partner?'

'Well . . .' I maintain the appearance of calm though my heart is beating wildly. I did not plan for this. How do I get around it?

'Can I expect to meet your partner soon, Mr Gallo? It is *Mr* Gallo, isn't it?'

I do not answer, too puzzled by his tone, wondering if it is merely his accent that confuses me.

He scrutinizes me carefully. 'I must tell you that a biologically *female* partner is necessary to bear the child. While there have been a few successful cases of hormonally treated men being implanted with embryos, you'd hardly want to take that risk with such special embryos as these.'

'Indeed,' I say. It is all I can do not to let my breath rush out in an enormous sigh of relief.

'If you have no woman in your life,' Mihalovich goes on, 'well, that need not be an obstacle. We can find you a surrogate mother for the implantation. That will add to the cost, of course. But I can assure you it's worth it. We have superior results.' He rises, looking out the window in his office door. 'I believe I can show you what I mean, presently.'

There is a rap at the door. I open it and see a small girl with glossy honey-coloured hair. The exact image of Sabrina in toddlerhood. Behind her is a tall, wan, blond woman.

Mihalovich tells me, 'This is my granddaughter. Just taking her first steps, as you can see. Observe her. Is she not perfect? A test-tube baby with some differentiation of genes. You have options to select hair and eye colour. We chose to make her eyes to green, to match her mother's. Surrogate mother, that is. You could have her hair made redder, to resemble yours.' He indicates my wig. 'You may also opt to have hormone therapy given to her later to increase her height and speed her physical development. As the specimen the egg was taken from was a Eurasian, lags in these areas are to be expected. But I'm sure you can see that she is already as lovely as she is.'

'She is,' I say.

The girl is grave and quiet, with none of Sabrina's lively spirit at that age. She looks over her shoulder at me curiously as her mother leads her up the stairs, so like and yet so unlike Sabrina. I say to Mihalovich, 'I wonder if I might meet her biological mother? So that I may be certain what she will be like when she grows up?'

'That is not possible,' Mihalovich says. 'The woman donated her eggs and left the country. I don't know where she is now.' I start to get to my feet. 'But,' Mihalovich adds smoothly, 'I can show you her picture, of course, and those of our other donors, though this is the superior one—why else would I choose her for my daughter's child?'

'I'd also like to see records of genetic tests, just to assure myself—' I indicate my twisted form. 'If it weren't for this I'd prefer to have a biological child, naturally.'

'You will be able to view the microscan of the embryos before implantation. But for now—' He hands me a folder marked M-16253.

As soon as I see that code I know. M-16 may merely have been a code they invented, but the date 25-3 will ever be engraved in my mind, for it should have been my wedding day.

'No taking of photographs, please,' he reminds me as I open it.

'Of course.' I say as casually as I can. I will myself to control the shaking of my hand as I go through the materials in the folder. There is a full-length photograph of Sabrina, plus vaccination certificates and a page of lab tests, printed in Cyrillic with English translations for the names of the tests in parentheses. 'All from legitimate clinics,' Mihalovich assures me, unfazed by the irony of it.

I will myself to commit the names of the clinics to memory. I intend to go and question them. I take my time scanning the data, then slowly close the folder.

'Would you care to see another?' he asks. I shake my head in reply. 'Then you agree with me that this is an excellent specimen? You only want the best for your child, I'm sure. Feel free to take your time deciding; I know it's an important decision,' Mihalovich says. Then he adds, 'Don't wait too long, though. We have limited eggs available. She's a limited edition model, you might say.'

I am anxious to go and begin my questioning of the clinics. It seems to be all I can do now. I am about to rise when a loud voice makes me jump. 'Dr Mihalovich, emergency!'

A man in a white lab coat appears on the screen of the computer on Mihalovich's desk. He says, 'We need your decision on what to do with the patient.'

Mihalovich speaks sharply in his language, and the man on the screen switches as well, slowly and laboriously.

I continue to stare. The voice was that of a stranger, yet there was something familiar about it. Then I realize it is the accent. It sounds Filipino. The doctor's hair was black, unusual in this country. A Filipino doctor in this remote corner of Eastern Europe? We do travel everywhere.

Mihalovich then turns to me and holds out his hand. 'It appears I have some business to attend to. I hope to hear from you soon.'

I leave, determined to go make discreet inquiries at the labs. But as I zip off on my scooter, I am assailed with doubt.

It has been two years. Would they remember her? I doubt Mihalovich used her actual name. Did he use his own name, even? Most likely he covers the traces of his illegal activities with aliases. The use of his name in his actual lab is for the sake of prestige, but when you think about it, risky.

Then I remember that sudden call. A patient, they said. Why would Mihalovich be concerned with a patient? They didn't say his wife or his son or anything like that but that cold impersonal term. Yet he was responsible for this person, for some reason.

I jerk the scooter to a stop in front of my apartment building and drag myself up the stairs to my room. On a hunch, I search online for hospitals, earmarking those that are known for their cancer research facilities. In a previous job I had learned that fertility drugs tend to increase the incidence of cancer. Our vaccines had not yet been tested on humans, and certainly not for those on fertility drugs. That might explain the cancer vaccine connection. I scan each hospital website. The name Herronimmo Ilagan leaps out of one hospital's list of medical staff, seeming to me vaguely familiar, though I can't seem to place it. I go on searching. I see Spanish, Chinese, and Filipino names listed elsewhere, most mere residents. This Ilagan appears to be the only one in a prominent position. And then I remember referring to his data on cancer patients during my bout at Arik's lab. The Arik connection again. He must be the one. I make a quick stop at my roommate's closet, put on one of his scrub suits and speed to the hospital.

At the hospital, I scan the cars in the parking lot nervously, hoping Mihalovich isn't there. I enter and find the cancer research division. I also find a cart loaded with medical supplies to push. My heart is pounding as I go past the nurse at the desk. I pray she won't look up. But she does. She speaks to me in her language. I understand not a word. I just nod dumbly, then continue on my way. When I am certain she is not following me, I release my breath at last.

I peek into every room. Most are occupied by older patients. A few are middle-aged. Then there is one room where a small, thin figure lies in a bed, with a few remaining locks of honey-coloured hair spread on her pillow.

I slip quietly into the room and kneel by the bed. At last, for the first time in two years, I am alone with the girl that I planned to marry.

I suppose there is little beauty left in her wasted body. But all I can think as I look at her, with her delicate bones and nearly translucent skin, that she looks like an otherworldly being. She is so light now that I am certain I can carry her away, disabled as I am, equipped only with a scooter. I touch her hand and shed my wig.

Her eyes flicker open. 'Frankl,' she mouths. She reaches up weakly and touches my face.

'Yes, here I am at last,' I say. I kiss her tenderly, then straighten up. 'I'm getting you out of here,' I tell her.

Very slightly she shakes her head. 'Impossible,' she murmurs. Her hand closes on mine with surprising strength.

We soon find that we are both right. In a moment, she is gone.

I stay beside her lifeless body longer than I should. Nobody comes in response to the alarm of her flatlined monitor. I suppose they had been instructed not to take the trouble of keeping her alive.

I leaf through the chart at the foot of her bed and find in brief the sad details of her last illness. Cancer, of course. Following radiation therapy, her benign tumour had shrunk but had later reincarnated itself as a malignant mass. I am disturbed to find that there was no drug therapy given. Nothing had been done to help her until these last few months, though it was indicated that the mass must have grown and metastasized over almost a year. Had they kept her imprisoned to harvest her eggs until she became too ill and weak for them to bother with her? And then they shunted her off to this facility to die alone. In my rage, I pull the chart of the clipboard, set to tear it up, then think better of it and stuff the papers in my pocket for evidence. I hold on to the foot of the bed, trembling as I look at her.

For a moment I am consumed with the wild idea of pushing Sabrina out on a stretcher and taking her with me— but where? How? Surely I would be caught. Sadly, I concede that I have no choice but to leave alone and that immediately. I stand up, stuffing the wig in my pocket. I touch her cheek one last time and pick up some strands of her golden-brown hair that had fallen on the pillow. I wind them around my ring finger as I slip out of the room. I hear footsteps echoing down the hall, so I slip around the corner and leave through the fire escape.

I stop at my apartment just long enough to pack a few essentials, strip myself of my prosthetic ear and throw it and my wig in the garbage chute, and bundle myself up in an oversized trench coat. Mihalovich may no longer be in the good graces of the government, but he could have his own spies or thugs to go after me. He could even bribe an officer. I've gathered in the two years I've been here that corruption is rampant around here.

I make it to the station without incident, though. On the train, I curl up in a seat, pretending to be asleep. But I know when the train stops at the border and some military officers come, probably looking for me. They shake my shoulder and I rouse myself long enough to show them my passport. Then I lean back. When they leave the train, I allow myself a sigh of relief.

9

Despite the great distance I must travel, my instinctual behaviour is to return home. For some days I do nothing, too dazed by grief as well as the rigors of travel. Then I rouse myself, knowing what I must do. I must get on with my life, of course, find work or a research grant somewhere. But first I must report everything I know to the international authorities. I make copies of the charts and go to the library to have Wendy print out the articles on Mihalovich.

'I hope you don't mind my asking, Frankl, but why are you so interested in this man?' she asks me over the hum of the printer. 'You're not doing . . .this kind of work, are you?'

I lean on my cane with one hand and catch the pages issuing out the machine with the other. 'What do you think?' I ask.

'I wouldn't believe such a thing of you,' she says. 'You know, no matter what it is, you can tell me, Frankl.'

I look at her. Though she is not afflicted with the same genetic aberration as Sabrina, I have always seen her as a child, too long have I known her as one. And her fragile appearance makes her seem even more child-like than Sabrina was. But I do feel the need to unburden myself and she is an old friend who was Sabrina's friend too. 'I can't tell you now. Not here,' I say. There are few others around, but a prolonged conversation between us, no doubt an emotional conversation given the topic, would arouse curiosity.

'I can take a break,' she offers.

I pay for my pages and we leave the nearly-empty library together. The library is on the edges of the community and close by is the grassy slope where Sabrina and I lay talking of our dreams our last night together. It is a gentle slope, but I know Wendy with her wheelchair could not manage it, besides I, with my limp, had had to lean on Sabrina's shoulder. In any case, it would have made it harder for me to keep my emotions under control to speak of her in that place despite the very different circumstances and time of day. Instead, I sit on a large tree root, which puts my face about level with Wendy's, though I cannot look her in the eyes when I tell her briefly about Mihalovich and what he had done to Sabrina. I hear rather than see her weep. I reach for her hand. I am weeping too.

They investigate, and Mihalovich is arrested. When the case is ready to come to trial, a lawyer contacts me and tells me the whole story. Sabrina was kidnapped when the plane was detained. Mihalovich had made a fake bomb threat and exploited his military connections to get Sabrina. She was then taken to Arik to receive cancer vaccines to prevent the risks of the radiation treatment that would remove her tumour and allow her body to develop normally following aggressive hormone therapy. Mihalovich paid Arik a handsome price for that, but not as great as the price she paid. The vaccines didn't work, obviously. But I guess he harvested as many of her eggs as he could until her failing health made the production of viable ones impossible. And having gotten what he needed from her, he found her too much trouble to keep and left her to die.

Although I am faithfully present at every session of the trial, I soon grow impatient with the length of time it takes. I listen intently to each witness, not bothering to conceal the rage on my face. What I still can't understand is why, why her? Was it really so rare for a child to be born beautiful and whole in the post-War world, even after so long? And how did they even know about her and her trip to Europe? Her father has maintained his innocence.

I get the answers, along with the surprise of my life, when my sister Brisa is called as a witness.

Upon hearing the name, I scan the vast room, and see a woman in a well-fitting suit and with gleaming highlights in her hair march to the stand. It's Brisa, but I barely recognize her, and not just because of the hair. Her figure seems trimmer somehow, her nose more prominent, and she wears no glasses. As she takes her seat, the video screen shows her larger than life for the benefit of the audience. She glances at her image and pushes her glossy hair over her shoulder with a smile. It's then that I realize her left-hand looks different. All the fingers are now whole.

The prosecutor's questions put a stop to her simpering. What did she have to do with the whole business? She is soon

compelled to describe her actions under oath. 'I informed
Mihalovich about my friend, Sabrina. I knew about him
and his work from my boyfriend, who used to work with
him abroad.'

As the questioning goes on, it is revealed that Brisa
informed Mihalovich of my pact with Sabrina, though I had
sworn my family to secrecy regarding this. I had never even
directly told Brisa about our engagement, but my mother
did. I can't blame her. I myself told Brisa that I was going
back to search for her, didn't I?

How could she have done this? Just because we never got
along didn't mean she had to be so disloyal. I can hardly bear
to look at her, even if she looks better than ever. Watching
her on the screen, I realize that she has managed to have her
teeth fixed and her nose lifted. When the prosecutor holds
up photographs for her to identify, she doesn't even squint.
She must have had laser eye surgery done. All this work,
along with having new fingers being grown from her stumps,
cannot have come cheaply. Her motive is obvious and I am
disgusted by her pettiness.

She looks at me from the stand without the slightest
remorse. In fact, when she looks at me there is a definite
look of triumph on her face. She has finally bested me in
something.

I know it will be a long time before I can return home
again.

The trial ends with Mihalovich being found guilty. Varied
sentences are also dealt out to his accomplices, which include
Arik. Brisa goes free, having made a deal for her testimony.
She claimed that she had no idea that Sabrina's life would be

endangered. I believe her, knowing how little she has kept up with genetic research despite being the daughter of a scientist. Still, I cannot forgive her.

But at least Mihalovich is finally behind bars. The eggs, sperm, and embryos he had in his possession were confiscated and placed in a freezer facility in the U.S. which is maintained for the embryos of endangered species. So Sabrina's genetic matter will neither be destroyed nor experimented with, and will only be used if the human race itself becomes an endangered species.

Soon after the trial, I retreat to a cottage in the foothills of the French Alps, which was awarded to me along with a research grant. It is one of many old rustic dwellings that were abandoned in the beginning of the last century as people migrated to cities. They were repopulated by refugees during the War then abandoned again as the cities were rebuilt. Being historic structures, they were acquired by the government and outfitted with modern facilities and given to people on research grants, like me. Despite the effect on my joints, I'm quite used to the chill of mountain air. I feel at home here. I feel it is just the place to raise a family. In spite of everything, I feel I might want to, someday.

10

Someday begins a few years later. Having settled into my new life, I decide it is time. I have met some of the women researchers here, and in certain seasons the nearby village is full of tourists who come to ski in the area. Margret came once to stay for a short-term grant, and a year later she and

Jac had their honeymoon in the village. I will not say it was because of their constant prodding that I thought of seeking love again. Still, I suppose seeing their happiness together stirred the longing for companionship that I had buried upon the death of Sabrina.

I have not developed close ties with those around me here, however. I feel I need someone who means home to me. And I find myself thinking more and more about Wendy. I have kept in touch with my old friend. She is not the same as Sabrina. But I care for her. She is a lovely girl, with a beautiful soul, and I feel I can do her some good, for she is all alone now. I send her a message, offering her a job as a research assistant, and her answer is yes.

I do my best for her. We look into getting her condition repaired. The options are horrifying though, even more horrifying than the possibilities for me, necessitating amputation of her twisted legs to be replaced by prosthesis connected to a system of microchips and wires that must be inserted in her spinal column through invasive surgery. Instead, I decide to get the best electric wheelchair for her, one that climbs the slopes so easily that it's work for me to catch up when I'm on foot.

Once settled into the extra bedroom in my cottage, she works on organizing my research data. We both know, though, that I had other reasons for sending for her. I could easily have gotten a student from a nearby university as my assistant.

Despite my delight in her efficiency, at first personal relations between us are somewhat awkward because the main bond we share is our past, and we are not comfortable talking too much about either Brisa or Sabrina. But we do share a love of learning, and delight in research. I soon find I think more clearly when I discuss things with her. I need her to listen to my ideas, to assure me they make sense. Even if she doesn't understand my work that well, her quiet assurance motivates me.

After some months, I am certain. I ask her to marry me. I wonder if she says yes out of mere gratitude, but she assures me that she loves me and agrees to my plan wholeheartedly. I am thankful, for now, we have Serena.

She is not much trouble, our Serena. We take turns looking after her. Wendy now works a shift in the village library, in between helping me with my records and adding to her files for a book on the War she hopes to write someday. I encourage her to be active since she enjoys it, but in my heart, I hate it—I've gotten so I find it hard to concentrate when she's not around. I have come to depend on her presence.

Serena still sleeps most of the day. But when she awakens she reaches for me and smiles and gurgles. Her eyes are blank and unseeing, but she knows I am there. It is probable her eyes will be operable when she is older, so we do not mind about them now. She has hair, to my relief, Wendy's thick waves. Her skin is creamy and her body is straight, though one leg is shorter than the other. Nothing that can't be remedied in the future. As yet, it is no inconvenience to her. I carry her in my arms, marvelling at her beauty, and count her fingers and toes. Ten each. She is perfect, as far as we are concerned.

I then go back to work, my motivation refuelled. I remember that I am trying to remove the taint that has made so many of the people of the world fearful of having children, that I am trying to find a means to prevent the myriad genetic defects that proliferated after the War from being passed on. There must be some way—a just way, without egg trafficking and cloning—that people, Wendy and myself included, can once again take it for granted that they will have children who are naturally free of serious defects.

We could have waited till then, I suppose, to have our daughter. But we are glad we have her now. Our lives would surely not be the same without her. Our treasure, our Serena.

Beautiful and whole.

#

Acknowledgments

The story "Virtual Centre" won first place in the Futuristic Fiction category in the Palanca Awards in 2002. I would like to thank the judges, chaired by Wendell Capili, for their selection of my story that led to my first major win that encouraged me to continue writing in the same vein. All the stories that follow the title one owe their existence to the first's encouraging win, as well as to Dean and Nikki Alfar's promotion of speculative fiction in my country. Even if I rarely could make the deadlines of their anthologies, just knowing that there was interest in Filipino sci-fi kept me writing it. I'm very grateful to all the teachers who have considered the early version of this story as worthy of inclusion in the twenty-first century Philippine literature curriculum, especially Gemino Abad and Marikit Uychoco who selected it for their anthologies.

Thanks to my teacher, Charlson Ong, who gave me such helpful advice when he workshopped 'The Beautiful and the Whole' in my first master's in creative writing class. Also my classmates Jenette, Hammed, Raymond, Paulo, Karen, Mo, Catherine, and Mabek, who read it and commented on it, even as it grew well past short story length, and to Paolo Manlapaz, Lorie Santos, Gerry Los Baños, and Emil Flores for commenting on it as well. Thanks, too, to Prof. Neil Garcia, who motivated me to improve the story "Hatchling".

Though they are no longer with us, I remember with gratitude my father who passed on his love of Ray Bradbury to me and therefore the desire to emulate him in a Philippine context, and my mother who urged me to try writing every kind of fiction.

Many thanks to Honey de Peralta for her helpful advice in preparing my submission and just for believing in me and my work, and to Nora Nazerene Abu Bakar for her insightful comments.

Most of all, I thank my husband Joel, who has been with me and supported me throughout my journey as a writer, and our three children who have always been my cheerleaders, even when as now they can't read my stories. Their belief in me is the purest, for which I am grateful. I humbly hope it is justified.